"It's not you that I'm afraid of, okay? It's...this place."

He was silent behind her. But his fingers moved lightly against her stomach. Almost as if he were caressing her.

"We're safe."

Her gaze slid to the right. His gun was there. Within easy reach. "Sometimes, I don't ever feel safe." As soon as she said the words, Noelle wished that she could call them back. She'd never made that confession to anyone.

"Why not?" His hold tightened.

Noelle shook her head. She was feeling warmer, so much warmer now. The shivers and shudders were easing. "Because I'm never sure what waits in the darkness."

WAY OF THE SHADOWS

New York Times Bestselling Author
CYNTHIA EDEN

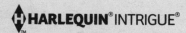

Recycling programs for this product may not exist in your area.

A big thanks to Denise and Shannon at Harlequin Intrigue—thank you so much for giving me the opportunity to write about the Shadow Agents.

For my wonderful readers…thank you for all the support that you've given to the men and women of the EOD. I hope that you've enjoyed their tales!

ISBN-13: 978-0-373-74837-2

WAY OF THE SHADOWS

Copyright © 2014 by Cindy Roussos

Printed in U.S.A.

www.Harlequin.com

ABOUT THE AUTHOR

New York Times and *USA TODAY* bestselling author Cynthia Eden writes tales of romantic suspense and paranormal romance. Her books have received starred reviews from *Publishers Weekly*, and she has received a RITA® Award nomination for best romantic suspense novel. Cynthia lives in the Deep South, loves horror movies and has an addiction to chocolate. More information about Cynthia may be found on her website, www.cynthiaeden.com, or you can follow her on Twitter, www.twitter.com/cynthiaeden.

Books by Cynthia Eden

CAST OF CHARACTERS

Thomas Anthony—For years, Thomas has carefully guarded his past. He's a man with secrets...and deadly killing talents. He's an EOD agent, and his job is to protect his country, to always complete his missions. But when one mission from his past comes back to haunt him, his finely held control begins to crack....

Noelle Evers—When it comes to killers, Noelle is an expert. As an FBI profiler, Noelle knows how to get right into the mind of a killer. However, it is Noelle's own mind that is a bit of a mystery to her. She was kidnapped and attacked fifteen years ago, but the days of her abduction have been lost from her memory. She is determined to unlock her past and to discover just why the mysterious Thomas Anthony seems connected to the most harrowing experience of her life.

Bruce Mercer—His business involves secrets—learning them, keeping them or exploiting them. The director of the EOD, he knows that life isn't always black-and-white. Sometimes, a good man has to commit dark deeds. When Noelle begins probing into her shadowed past, he realizes that secrets he has fought to keep for years are about to be brought out into the harsh light of day.

Lawrence Duncan—Senator Duncan has spent years amassing his power, and he doesn't plan to stand idly by while someone tries to destroy him. He knows that if the truth about his past is ever discovered, he will lose everything...and that is why the senator will do *anything* to protect himself from the EOD's investigation.

Paula Quill—As Senator Duncan's assistant, Paula has spent the past few years making herself invaluable to him. Their relationship has grown intimate, but...does Paula know just how dangerous the senator truly is? Paula may not be as innocent as she seems. In a life-and-death battle, trusting the wrong person could prove to be a fatal mistake.

Prologue

The darkness was all she knew. It surrounded her, seemed to suffocate her. It bound her as deeply, as securely as the ropes around her wrists.

Fear coiled around Noelle Evers as she waited in the dark. She was waiting for her own death, and she knew it. That certainty was there, filling her mind—that and nothing else. So when the door opened and she heard the squeak of wood, Noelle tensed.

The light spilled forward. The wood squeaked again.

Someone was coming toward her....

The beam of a flashlight slit through her eyes, blinding her because it was such a sharp contrast to the darkness.

"Found her!" A man's voice called. It was deep and rough, heavy with relief. "She's alive!"

Noelle squinted as she tried to see past that bright light.

More footsteps thudded toward her. Then hands were on her. Rough, strong hands. They pulled at her ropes then yanked her out of the chair and to her feet.

"It's all right," that deep, rumbling voice told her. "You're safe now."

She didn't believe him.

There were more lights then, sweeping into the room. It looked like…a cabin? She was in a cabin? In the darkness, she hadn't been able to tell anything about her surroundings, but she could now see glimpses of an old, log-lined cabin.

She licked her lips. Her mouth felt so dry. She had to swallow three times before she managed, "H-how did…I g-get here?"

His face was in shadows, but he was tall, with broad shoulders and a gun strapped to his hip.

Noelle backed up when she saw the weapon. Her feet slipped on something. She glanced down and saw a twisting mass of rope near her feet.

"Easy," he told her, and his grip tightened around her arms. "I'm a deputy. We're all with the Coleman County Sheriff's Department, and we're here to take you home."

She'd…she'd been at home…sleeping in her

bed….Noelle remembered that. She'd gone to sleep—and awoken to darkness.

"Sheriff!" Another voice cried out then, breaking with what sounded like fear.

The deputy pulled Noelle close as he hurried toward that cry.

The flashlights all hit the far left corner of the room. They fell on the man sprawled there. A man who was dead—his throat had been cut. The man stared sightlessly back at them while his blood formed a dark pool beneath him.

The deputy's hold on Noelle tightened. "Who is that?" he demanded.

Noelle started to shake.

"Ms. Evers…" His voice gentled a bit. "Is he one of the men who took you?"

Tears leaked down her cheeks. "I don't know!"

Voices rose. Shouted. More men and women came inside the cabin. More lights.

Too bright.

Noelle's shoulders hunched. She looked down at her wrists. They were bloody and raw. And her hands—her hands were stained with blood. So was her gown. The gown she'd worn to sleep when she climbed into her own bed.

This isn't my home. But she couldn't remember how she'd gotten there. Noelle only knew darkness.

The deputy pulled off his coat. Carefully, he put it around her shoulders. "Tell me what happened." He was leading her from the cabin keeping his fingers around her arm. "Get me a medic!" He called out to another one of the men swarming the area.

Then she was outside. The night air was crisp, but she could still smell blood.

Because it's on me.

"I want to go home," Noelle whispered. "I want to see my parents." Noelle was seventeen. She was a sophomore at Coleman High School. She was cheering at the football game on Friday. She was—

Noelle's knees gave way and she would've hit the ground if the deputy hadn't grabbed her. He lifted her up against his chest, holding her tightly. *"Medic!"* the deputy yelled.

She wasn't just shaking any longer. Noelle's eyes rolled back in her head as giant shudders jolted through her.

The deputy carried her to a gurney. He and the medic strapped her down. "What the hell is happening?"

"Noelle!" She heard the scream distantly, but she knew that voice. It was her mother's voice. Noelle tried to respond, but she couldn't speak.

"She's seizing," the medic snapped. "We need to get her stable!"

The darkness seemed to close in again. She didn't want to go back into the dark.

Something bad waited in the dark.

Death waited.

But Noelle couldn't fight, and the darkness took her once more.

THE NEXT TIME Noelle's eyes opened, she was surrounded by a sea of white. The scent of antiseptic told her she was in the hospital even before the room came into focus.

She blinked a few times then saw her mother's tear-filled gaze. "You're okay, baby," her mom whispered.

Noelle didn't feel okay.

"We need to ask her some questions."

Noelle's gaze darted to the left at those words. Her father stood close by. He looked pale, and...older than she'd ever seen him.

Right next to her father, Sheriff Morris Bartley stood, his stare on her. He leaned toward Noelle.

"She just woke up," her father gritted out.

"I know." The sheriff sighed. "But she's the only one who can tell us what happened. I got a dead body, and I got her and I need to know—"

The darkness waited.

Noelle gave a hard, negative shake of her head.

"Noelle, how did you wind up in that cabin?" the sheriff asked her.

"This needs to wait," her father barked.

The machines around Noelle began to beep, faster, louder.

"Who was the dead man? Is he the one who took you? Is he—"

"I don't remember," Noelle whispered. Her throat hurt. *She* hurt.

The sheriff exhaled on a rough sigh. His hands gripped his hat. "Start with what you know. Tell me who took you from your house. Tell me how you got to that cabin and how—"

"I don't remember." Her voice was even softer now.

The sheriff's brows shot up. "Did you leave your house willingly? Is that what happened? Did you—?"

He didn't understand. "I don't…remember anything."

Her mother gave a little gasp.

"I was in my room, in my bed." Noelle's heart galloped in her chest. The machines raced. "Then I was in the dark." She blinked away the tears that filled her eyes.

Something happened in the dark. Something bad.

"I don't remember," she said again, and it was almost as if…as if the words were a vow.

The machines beeped louder around her. Noelle's mother pulled Noelle into a tight hug.

And, over her mother's shoulder, Noelle glanced up and met the eyes of the sheriff. There was concern in his gaze and suspicion.

I don't remember.

There was only darkness in her mind, and Noelle didn't know if that was good...or bad.

Chapter One

Fifteen years later...

The plane dipped, hitting another hard patch of turbulence, and Noelle Evers locked her fingers around the armrest on either side of her body. The private plane was currently flying over an area of pure-white land in Alaska, and Noelle was afraid they might be diving right *into* that snowy landscape at any moment.

"Relax," a low, gravel-rough voice told her. "We'll be landing in just a few more minutes."

The voice—and the guy who went with that voice—pulled Noelle's attention from the narrow window. She looked at the man seated directly across from her.

Thomas Anthony.

Tall, dark, deadly...and, currently, her partner on this assignment. Thomas "Dragon" Anthony was a man who seemed to always put her on edge.

"If you're going to be working with the EOD," Thomas murmured as he lifted one dark eyebrow, "rough flights will be the least of your worries."

Noelle forced herself to take a long, deep breath. She didn't want to show any weakness in front of Thomas. The man made her far too...nervous. Too *aware*.

Noelle was new to the EOD—the Elite Operations Division. She'd been recruited by EOD Director Bruce Mercer a few months back. Normally, the agents in that secretive group were all ex-military. They belonged to some of the most elite military units operating in the world. The agents were recruited to join the EOD because of their skills and because they were deadly when it came to their missions.

Noelle wasn't ex-military. She didn't specialize in killing or hunting prey. Instead, her specialty was getting *inside* a killer's mind. Before Bruce Mercer had used his pull to get Noelle into the EOD, she'd been working as a profiler at the FBI.

But then one of the EOD agents had gone rogue...and Mercer had brought her in to profile the agents there.

To hunt a killer within the division.

"You don't fit, you know," Thomas added in

that deep, dark voice of his. A voice that made her tense and think of things she really shouldn't.

The plane bounced again. Noelle swallowed. "You mean because I lack the military training?"

"I mean because when we get into a life-or-death situation—and we will—you won't be prepared to take the necessary action."

Her eyes narrowed at those words. *Way to insult your partner on the first case.* "Look, I might not be an ex–Army Ranger—" as *he* was "—but I worked at the FBI for five years. I've been in plenty of dangerous situations, and I've handled myself just fine."

Thomas's lips quirked a bit. They were sensual lips, with a faintly cruel edge. Thomas was a handsome man, if you went for the deadly, dangerous type. As a general rule, Noelle definitely did *not* go for that type. She preferred safe guys, with a capital *S*.

And everything about Thomas spelled *DANGER*. From the top of his midnight-black hair down to his well-worn hiking boots, the guy just oozed a threat. Maybe it was because she'd read his file. She knew just what he was capable of doing—what he *had* done. Thomas didn't need any weapon when he went after his targets. He could kill—and had—quite easily, with his hands. He'd earned the nickname of Dragon while at the EOD because he was a martial-arts expert—he attacked with brutal control, and his opponents never had a chance against him.

Cold. Hard. Dangerous.

Thomas had a firm, square jaw, a blade-sharp nose and sculpted cheekbones that gave him a strong, fierce appearance. His deep, golden eyes reminded her of a lion's gaze. Maybe because every time she looked into those eyes, Noelle felt as if he were a predator and she was his prey.

We're partners. Partners. Mercer had sent them on this trip to Alaska because they were supposed to be hunting a killer. Together.

"You've never killed anyone," Thomas said as he tilted his head to study her. "Death is a way of life for EOD agents."

"Yes, well, I'm sure this will shock you, but FBI agents see plenty of death, too." Death was rather her specialty. "I know killers, and you can trust me to do my job."

Her job... Her job was to question the suspect they were pursuing. To break through the very public façade the man presented and to determine if Alaskan Senator Lawrence Duncan was the man who'd recently plotted the destruction of the EOD.

Thomas's eyes narrowed just a bit as he gazed at her.

And there it is again. He was looking at her with a touch of familiarity. As if he knew her.

Too well.

But Noelle hadn't met Thomas Anthony until she started work at the EOD just a few months before. They were most certainly not intimately acquainted.

No matter how Thomas might glance at her.

"You're doing it again," Noelle blurted. Then she could have bitten her tongue when his face tensed. She was normally so much better at controlling her emotions and her responses to people, but Thomas just put her on edge.

"Doing what?" Thomas asked voice totally emotionless.

"Staring at me…as if—as if we're—" She floundered because what Noelle really wanted to say was…*As if we're lovers.* But they weren't. No way would she have forgotten him.

It was just…the intensity in his eyes…the heat…

"I make you nervous," he said.

Why lie? "Yes."

"Because you know what I've done." His gaze slid to the files on the seat beside her. "You read all of our files, right? When you were trying to decide which EOD agent was actually a psychotic killer in disguise."

That had been her *first* assignment at the EOD. This outing to Alaska was her second.

"So, what's the verdict, doc?" The *doc* was mocking, but Noelle was a doctor, a psychiatrist. She'd been trying for years to understand the demons that chased people.

Ever since she'd woken up in a small, southern hospital with her life shattered around her.

"Tell me…" Thomas continued with his gaze assessing. "Am I dangerous? Am I psychotic? Is that why you tense up every time I get near you?" He leaned forward. "Are you afraid I'll hurt you?" Then, before she could respond, his jaw hardened even more. "Because that's not the way things work at the EOD. You trust your partner, or you don't trust anyone."

She couldn't seem to take a deep enough breath. Thomas filled the space around her so completely.

The pilot's voice floated over the intercom then, announcing their impending landing.

Thomas leaned back.

But Noelle's hand flew out. She touched his wrist.

Thomas stilled.

"I know you're not psychotic. You're a soldier. A damn fine one, at that," she added

because it was true. "And if I seem nervous…"
Tell him. "It's not you, really. I have a…very
hard time getting close to people." Mostly because Noelle had made a habit of putting a wall
between herself and others.

Once, that wall had been necessary for
Noelle's survival. But now, she didn't know
how to live without that protection.

His gaze dropped to her hand.

Noelle slowly pulled her fingers back.

After a moment, Thomas's stare lifted once
more to her face. "You'll be closer to me than
you will be to anyone else."

Goose bumps rose on Noelle's arms. Was
that a promise? Or a warning?

Then the plane began its descent, and she
held back the other questions she wanted to
ask him.

THOMAS ANTHONY WAS used to danger. He was
used to pain. He was used to surviving any and
every hellhole on earth. As an Army Ranger,
his job had been to get the mission accomplished, no matter what.

But his job had never involved working intimately with Noelle Evers, not until now.

She doesn't remember me.

He'd known that, of course, from the beginning. From the first day he'd glanced up at the

EOD and found himself staring into her warm, hazel eyes. Just looking at her had been like a punch to his gut. He'd wondered if she'd seen the flare of recognition in his eyes, but...

No, she hadn't shown any awareness of the past they shared.

That was a good thing. Her not remembering helped him. Because if she ever did remember what he'd done...

She'd be terrified of me.

Even more afraid than she already was.

And, despite her words, Noelle was afraid of him. Thomas knew a whole lot about fear, and he was certain of the emotion he saw in her eyes.

"The senator will see you now," Paula Quill said as she pointed toward the closed door on the right. The woman's blond hair was pulled back in a perfect twist, and her face was schooled to show not even a hint of curiosity about their visit. As the senator's assistant, Thomas figured the woman was used to keeping that mask of hers in place.

They were in the senator's mansion, a too-big, mausoleum-type place Thomas didn't like. But they'd needed to track the man back to his lair, even if that lair was in one of the most isolated spots in Alaska.

"He's waiting in his study," Paula added.

Paula was pretty, a woman in her early twenties, and based on what Thomas knew about the senator, Paula was *exactly* the guy's type. The senator was single, and from all accounts, quite a ladies' man.

The EOD also suspected the man was a killer.

Noelle breezed past the other woman and headed into the senator's study.

Noelle and Paula…they were night and day. Paula was icy reserve, cold perfection.

But Noelle…with her dark, red hair and her striking face…she was heat. Fire.

Passion.

The senator turned at Noelle's approach, a fake smile on his face. Senator Lawrence Duncan was forty-two, rich and currently the chief suspect in the recent bombing of the EOD office in Washington D.C.

Someone with a whole lot of power had hired an assassin—a man known as the Jack of Hearts—to take out EOD Director Bruce Mercer *and* to destroy the EOD in the process.

Right now, all of their intel was pointing to Senator Duncan as being that person in question.

"Senator Duncan." Noelle's voice was smooth, giving no hint at all to her southern roots.

"Thank you for seeing us today." She offered the senator her hand.

And he held it far too long. "How could I refuse?" Duncan murmured. "Though I'll confess, I don't quite know why the FBI wants to see me."

That was their cover. They were acting as FBI agents because even U.S. senators didn't have clearance to know about EOD missions.

But if this guy is the one we're after, he already knows far too much about the EOD.

"We have some questions to ask you," Noelle murmured. "About a killer who was recently hunting in D.C."

Paula pulled the door shut, sealing them inside the room with the senator as she left.

The senator's gaze swept over Noelle. He was still holding her hand and looking far too appreciative as his gaze dipped over her.

Noelle was a fine-looking woman, no doubt about it. Tall and curved, Thomas had seen plenty of men pass admiring stares her way. And every time those guys gazed at her with desire flaring in their eyes, Thomas wanted to drive his fist into their faces.

He cleared his throat. "I'm Agent Thomas Anthony," Thomas said. A full, fake dossier had been created with his FBI credentials, just in case the senator wanted to dig. "And we certainly appreciate your cooperation." Bull. Thomas didn't appreciate anything about the jerk, and if the guy didn't let Noelle's hand go in the next five seconds—

Noelle pulled away from the senator. "Are you familiar with the killer known as the Jack of Hearts?"

Duncan blinked. "Ah…I read about him in the paper. Wasn't he the serial killer who left playing cards at the scenes of his kills?"

Not exactly. Jack had been a murderer all right, but he'd been an assassin, not a serial killer. His kills hadn't been for pleasure. They'd been for pure profit.

"That's him," Noelle inclined her head toward the senator. Thomas noticed her gaze swept around the study.

Thomas followed her stare. Duncan was a hunter. The trophies from his kills filled the walls of the room. And so did pictures. Pictures of cabins. Of boats. Of smiling women who stood at his side.

"Ah, well, I've certainly never met the man." Duncan took a seat behind his desk. He motioned toward the couch on the right. "So I don't see how I can—"

"When the authorities caught up with him," Noelle interrupted smoothly. "He was planning to escape on your boat, the *Dreamer.* It was docked in D.C., and Jack had intended to slip away on that vessel."

The senator's eyes flared with surprise. "I hadn't realized that. I heard he was at the dock, but not that he was planning to use *my* boat."

Thomas thought the senator's response seemed a little too perfect. Almost rehearsed.

"Do you have any idea why he might have selected *your* boat?" Noelle didn't sit on the couch. Neither did Thomas. They both kept standing. Noelle pulled a photograph from the manila file she carried, and she pushed it across the desk toward the senator. "Take a look at Jack, and tell me...have you seen him before?"

The senator's gaze darted down to the photo, then right back to Noelle. "I see so many people on the campaign trail. Our paths could've crossed, and I wouldn't know it."

"Why did he choose *your* boat?" Thomas demanded because the senator had conveniently not answered that particular question.

Duncan's gaze—a dark brown—darted toward him. "Agent...Anthony, was it? I have no idea why he chose my boat. Perhaps it was just convenient for him. The right escape boat, at the right place."

Thomas wasn't buying that. "Before he died, the killer implied he knew you. That you'd *hired* him to do work for you in the past."

The senator's jaw hardened. "I have dozens of people working for me at any given time. You can check with Paula to see if this—this man was part of our extended staff, but I've certainly had no personal experience with him."

"I'm not talking about hiring him to work as part of your campaign team." Thomas knew his voice had roughened. He also knew Noelle was carefully studying the senator's reaction to their questions. "I'm asking if you hired him to kill for you."

The senator shot to his feet. "This is outrageous!" He pointed toward the door. "Leave. Now. I will not stand for this sort of harassment!"

"It's not harassment," Noelle said quietly. "It's just questioning. And we thought it would be better for you if we did that questioning here, away from prying eyes, instead of back in the limelight of D.C."

Anger burned in Duncan's stare. "Now I see why I warranted a *personal* visit from the FBI. It's certainly not every day that I'm tracked to my home like this…." His breath heaved out in what was probably supposed to look like an affronted rush. "I don't like the accusations flying from you two."

"We've made no accusations," Noelle replied. Thomas had to admire her. She was good at keeping her emotions in check. "We're simply asking you questions."

"You're *done* with your questions." The senator stomped toward the door. "You want to see me again, you talk to my lawyer." He yanked open the door and gave them a hard glare. "Hope you enjoy your trip back to D.C. By the time you get there, I'll have already talked to your supervisor. You'll both be lucky to have jobs waiting on you."

Oh, Thomas was sure the jobs would be waiting. He was also sure they wouldn't be leaving Alaska anytime soon.

The mission isn't over. It's just started.

"Thanks for your time, Senator," Noelle said. "It's certainly been enlightening."

Duncan frowned at that, but Noelle just headed right past the guy.

Thomas took his time following her. He'd been around men like the senator before. Men born with silver spoons shoved deep in their mouths. He often wished those guys would choke on them.

"You and your partner should be careful," the senator muttered. "This is a dangerous part of the country."

Thomas froze. Had that jerk just *threatened* them? He turned his head and met the senator's dark stare.

"No one comes into my home and tries to destroy me," the senator spat at him. "No one. You've just made a very powerful enemy."

Thomas fought the urge to roll his eyes. "Right. In case you can't tell, I'm terrified right now."

The senator frowned.

It was Thomas's turn to smile. "Something you should know, too. I'm a bit of a hunter, like you." He motioned to the trophies on the wall. "Only I don't hunt animals. I take out the humans who are too dangerous to be walking the streets."

"I—" The senator's face reddened.

Thomas leaned in closer to him. "We know what you did. We know what you are. Soon, the whole world will know, too."

The senator's shoulders hunched.

Thomas nodded. "We'll be seeing you again, soon." Because they hadn't come all the way to Alaska for some quick turnaround trip. They'd come to Alaska to get the proof they needed. Proof of the senator's guilt. They weren't leaving until they'd accomplished their mission.

Satisfied he'd made his point, Thomas exited behind Noelle. Paula watched them with wide, wary eyes. Thomas knew she'd overheard plenty of their conversation. *If you're smart, lady, you'll get away from the senator, as fast as you can.*

But Paula appeared to have frozen in place.

Thomas and Noelle didn't speak again until they'd left the senator's mansion. Once they were back inside their rented SUV, Thomas glanced at Noelle.

She was staring up at the senator's home.

"Don't keep me in suspense," he drawled as he cranked the vehicle. A light dusting of snow had started to fall. "What did you think?"

She didn't glance his way. "It's too early to tell."

He didn't buy it. Noelle made her living by reading people. By looking past the bright, shiny surface they presented to the rest of the world. He pulled out of the winding drive and headed back toward the cabin in town that the EOD had rented for them.

They hadn't bothered with getting a room in the local lodge—they'd needed more permanency.

They were planning to stay in Alaska for the long haul.

Until we can bury the senator.

"But I do know he was lying to us," Noelle added.

Thomas wasn't a profiler, and he knew that. The guy had barely been able to hold eye contact with him, and the senator had reacted far too strongly to their questions.

"So he's our guy." Thomas kept his hold steady on the steering wheel. He'd driven on snow-covered roads plenty of times. But those roads were sure different from the dirt roads of his youth.

"I think he could be. The man is controlling, dominating, and he's—" Noelle hesitated. "I think there may be quite a few layers to the senator."

"Yeah, well, your job is to peel away those layers, isn't it? To find out what hides underneath." That knowledge made him nervous. He didn't want Noelle to ever see beneath the surface he presented. Thomas had told her before she shouldn't profile him, but he'd caught her staring at him a few times, her eyes curious.

What does Noelle see when she looks at me? He knew what he saw when he looked into her eyes.

The thing I want most.

But when she stared at him, Thomas wondered if she just saw a killer.

Unfortunately, that was exactly what he was.

"THEY NEED TO VANISH," Lawrence Duncan said as his fingers tightened around the phone he had pressed to his ear. "Hell, yes, I know the risks, and that's why I'm telling you...*they can't make it out of this area.*"

His heart was racing in his chest. It had been pounding too fast from the moment his study door had opened and FBI agent Noelle Evers had walked inside. He'd recognized her instantly, even after all those long years. "She's a threat," he said flatly. "One that should have been eliminated by now."

Silence stretched on the phone line.

"Do it," Lawrence snarled. "Or I will." Even though he hated to get his hands dirty. But too much was at stake in this situation. They were already too exposed. And when Noelle put the pieces together—

I'll lose everything.

He heard the rough rasp of breathing on the other end of the line. Lawrence waited, hoping to hear—

"They'll die tonight."

He smiled. "The snowfall is just going to get heavier. They're on their way to their cabin now. That means they are heading *your* way." He'd taken the liberty of acquiring all of his information earlier. His assistant, Paula, had a knack for discovering information. Even before the agents had entered his home, Lawrence had known where they'd be staying in town.

"With weather like this, it will be easy enough for them to have an accident."

A fatal one.

The senator hesitated. "Just…don't leave obvious wounds on their bodies."

"Don't worry, there won't be any bodies to find."

The words should have chilled Lawrence, but he'd lost his conscience long ago. The first time he'd seen a kill, his life had changed.

And the blood had stained his hands ever since.

THEY'D BEEN DRIVING for about twenty minutes when the bright flash of headlights illuminated their rental vehicle. Thomas narrowed his eyes as he glanced in the rearview mirror. He could hear the growl of a fast-approaching vehicle behind him.

Even as the snow continued to fall in heavier waves.

"Where'd he come from?" Noelle asked as she turned in her seat to glance back.

Thomas's hands tightened around the wheel. Adrenaline spiked in his blood as the other vehicle's engine growled again and seemed to come even closer.

"What is he doing?" Alarm sharpened Noelle's

voice. "Maybe we should slow down, in case he wants to pass."

The road was narrow and surrounded by trees. Up ahead, an old bridge crossed over what looked like an ice-filled lake.

"We're not slowing down," Thomas said because his instincts were screaming at him. A dark road. A driver who was—

The other vehicle slammed into the back of Thomas's SUV. The impact was jarring, and he had to fight to keep the SUV from swerving off the road. "Hold on," he growled to Noelle. "Just hold—"

The other driver came at them again, hitting even harder this time. The SUV's wheels slipped on the icy road as the bridge loomed before them.

"It's a truck," Noelle gasped out. "I can see its outline. It's big and—"

It hit them again. Noelle's words ended in a scream because the SUV flew across the slick road. They were heading for the bridge. The SUV started to spin as the tires slid right over the ice.

"Thomas!"

The SUV slammed into the side of the bridge. The impact was on Noelle's side, and Thomas's gaze immediately jerked toward her as fear clawed through him.

Her hair had fallen over her face, and the echo of her scream seemed to shudder through his whole body. "Noelle?"

Thomas could hear the other vehicle's motor growling again. The SOB was going to come at him again. And if the truck hit them, they could easily plunge into the frigid water.

They had to get out of there, fast. "Come on, baby," he said, the endearment sliding from his mouth without thought because it was *her*. "We have to move."

The bright headlights were on them again. Coming fast, too fast.

Noelle's head lifted. She blinked at him. "Thomas?"

He yanked her free from the seat belt. He was already out of his, too. He shoved open his door.

The vehicle slammed right into Thomas's open door. Metal crunched, groaned—and the door ripped away as the truck drove their SUV harder into the side of the bridge and its old railing.

"Climb out the back!" Thomas yelled. "Hurry!" He pushed her into the rear seat. He had his weapon in his hands, and he turned back, aiming toward the other driver.

Who are you? What in the hell is happening?

His bullets blasted through the other vehicle's windshield. The truck stopped its advance. Noelle had made it into the backseat. She forced open the rear door, and Thomas followed her, barely fitting in the small escape space because the vehicle was wedged so closely to the railing.

He'd just cleared the vehicle when—

The truck hit them again. Only this time, the railing broke. Glass shattered. Metal crunched. And the wooden barrier splintered.

Thomas grabbed tightly to Noelle, and he lunged forward with her, hurtling them toward the woods near the edge of the bridge. They hit the snow and rolled down the ravine, tumbling again and again as they flew toward the bottom.

The SUV crashed into the frozen lake, sending chunks of ice into the air.

Thomas and Noelle finally stopped. They were about two feet away from that lake. Noelle was on top of him, and he quickly reversed their positions, holding her tightly. He could hear the growl of the other vehicle's engine, and then...

"He's leaving," Noelle whispered.

Yes, he was. Because he thought he'd gotten his prey?

The engine's snarl grew softer as the truck drove away.

The snow kept falling.

Noelle pushed against his shoulders. Thomas rose slowly, and he pulled Noelle to her feet. Their SUV was partially submerged and sinking fast. Damn it.

"Are you all right?" Thomas asked her as his eyes swept over her. He didn't see any injuries, but he wanted to be sure she was all right.

"He just tried to kill us!" She sounded incredulous.

She was also shaking.

Because it was cold out there. He shouldered out of his coat and pushed it toward her. When she tried to refuse, Thomas just wrapped it around her shoulders. "Senior agent," he snapped at her, still remembering the flash of fear he'd felt in the SUV. "That means you do what I say. Right now, I'm saying…*take my coat.*"

She pulled the coat closer. Thomas yanked out his phone. They'd rolled a good twenty feet from the road. A heavy darkness was already sweeping over the area. He lifted the phone— and realized it had been smashed to hell and back during the tumble.

"Tell me your phone's working," he said.

"I…I think it's in the SUV."

Hell.

The temperature was too low. It was getting too dark. No one was going to see them down there, and if anyone did happen to come along that lonely stretch of road again, it could very well be the same jerk who'd just tried to kill them.

Noelle started to climb back up toward the road. He caught her arm, stopping her. "Was your gun in the vehicle, too?" Thomas demanded.

She gave a grim nod. "Yours?" Noelle asked softly.

"You know I don't need a gun to kill." She was still shivering. They had to get to safety, fast. "But I've got the weapon."

"Stay to the shadows as much as possible," Thomas told her, keeping his voice quiet, too. In this area, any noise would carry easily. "He could come back, but we have to travel close to the road because running through the wilderness sure isn't an option for us." Not unless they wanted a slow death.

"I thought I saw a turnoff, a mile or so before the bridge," Noelle told him. When she spoke, a small cloud appeared before her mouth. *It's too cold out here.* "Maybe there's a cabin there. Someone who can help us."

Maybe. Right then, that turnoff sounded like their best chance. He kept his hold on her arm, and they started walking through the darkness.

Chapter Two

"You need to strip."

The cabin door slammed closed behind Noelle. At Thomas's growled words, Noelle stiffened. "Excuse me?"

They'd been walking for what felt like an hour. They'd taken the turnoff from the main road and slogged ahead until they'd found this place—a rundown, one-room cabin, which looked as if it hadn't been used in years.

It was as cold inside as it was outside. Noelle couldn't stop the shivers that rocked her body.

"Your core temperature is too low," Thomas told her flatly. "We have to get warm. The snow wet our clothing, so we have to ditch it." He was leaning over what looked like one very ancient fireplace. "Lucky damn night," he rasped. "There's some old wood here."

Uh, yeah, but how were they going to *light* that fire and—

He pulled out a small kit from his pocket and went to work. A flame flared seconds later.

Her breath expelled in a relieved rush.

Still kneeling in front of the fire, Thomas glanced back at her. "There was no way I'd come into the Alaskan wilderness without a fire kit."

She shivered. Again.

"Strip," he ordered once more.

The cabin was deserted, so they sure weren't going to get any rescue crew out there that night. But if they didn't warm up, soon, Noelle realized the odds of them making it until morning weren't going to be high.

Thomas headed toward her.

Noelle tensed.

"There you go again," he said, and he sounded angry. "When will you learn, I'm not going to bite?"

"I—"

He brushed by her and yanked open a small closet. No, he yanked *down* that closet's door; the old thing just literally fell off its hinges. "This will have to do for kindling 'cause we aren't finding any dry wood outside." He broke the door into heavy chunks. He had the fire flaring even higher when he added it. His back was turned to her as she inched toward that inviting warmth.

"My clothes are hitting the floor," Thomas told her bluntly. "Yours need to do the same."

Because they were soaked. But...

He stripped out of his sweater. Dropped the shirt he'd worn under it for layering. When he bent to remove his boots and socks, the firelight flickered over the tight muscles in his chest and arms. He had to work out—a lot. She'd never seen anyone with such sculpted muscles. As she stared at him—probably too long and too hard—Noelle could just make out the...scars on his body. Twisting, sharp, they snaked around his abs and lined his back.

She remembered the wound notations in his files. He'd been captured on a mission a while back. Held. Tortured. But, by the time rescue had come, all of his captors had been dead.

Thomas turned then. He still wore his jeans. His eyes met hers. "It's not personal," he told her in his deep, dark voice. "It's survival."

She felt her cheeks burn. Well, at least burning was better than freezing. Noelle fumbled and her clothes started to hit the floor. His jacket. Hers. Her sweater. Her undershirt. Her boots. Her socks.

Her fingers were fumbling, uncoordinated, as she tried to unhook the snap of her jeans.

"Let me." His voice was rougher than before, and his fingers were suddenly working at her waistband. He was so close, seeming to surround her with his strength. Noelle tried to pull in a deep breath, and his scent—masculine and crisp—wrapped around her.

Her zipper eased down with a hiss of sound.

She jerked back from him. Nearly fell. Would have, if Thomas hadn't snagged her arm so quickly. "Easy," he murmured.

Easy was the last thing she felt right then.

His fingers slowly uncurled their grip. "I'll spread out our clothes to dry. We should try to get some rest near the fire."

Noelle didn't hold out a lot of hope regarding rest. She bent and pushed her jeans down her legs. Then she looked up. Thomas had turned his back to her, but he'd stuck his hand out behind him, obviously waiting for her jeans. She pushed them into his hand.

"The rest," Thomas pressed.

"No way," Noelle said, aware that her voice held a sharp snap. "I'm keeping on my underwear, and I want you to do the same." Her panties and her bra were dry enough, and she was absolutely not planning to flash him any more than necessary.

Noelle thought she heard Thomas sigh, but he bent and finished spreading out her clothes. And his. And—

"Sorry," he said, voice a bit wry as she jerked

her gaze off him and back toward the fire. "But I'm not wearing underwear."

No, no, he *hadn't* been.

Noelle dropped toward the fire. She sat on the floor and pulled her knees up toward her. She was still shivering, and the tips of her fingers and toes were starting to ache.

A few moments later, Thomas eased down next to her. He reached for her.

The flinch was instinctive. She'd been withdrawing from people ever since—well, ever since she'd been seventeen years old and she'd woken, terrified, in a cabin that had actually looked a whole lot like the one they were currently in.

Her shoulders hunched.

"We need to share body warmth," he said again. "Don't worry I think I can control myself here."

Okay, now he was just mocking her.

But his hands gently curled around her, and he eased her fully down on the wooden floor next to him. Then he curled his body around hers. His left arm slid under her head, almost like a pillow, while his right curled around her stomach and pulled her back against the warm, hard cradle of his body.

"I *think* that I can," he added roughly, his breath blowing over the shell of her ear.

The fire crackled in front of her.

Noelle swallowed and tried to figure out what she was supposed to do in this situation. Being naked and trapped in a one-room cabin with Agent Thomas Anthony certainly hadn't been on her to-do list.

"I think we have confirmation of the senator's guilt."

His rumbling voice seemed to roll right through her.

"We visit the senator," Thomas continued grimly, "then less than half an hour later, some maniac tries to kill us. Connecting those dots sure isn't hard."

No, it wasn't, and Noelle had never been the type to believe in coincidences. She tried to put a little more space between their bodies.

Thomas just pulled her right back against him. "He left the scene because he thinks we're dead."

"If we hadn't cleared the SUV right then, we would be dead." Her own words were quiet and they gave no hint to the terror that had rocked through her as she fought to get out of the vehicle. As cold as it was outside…if they'd plunged beneath the ice in that lake, survival would have been only a dim hope. "But I don't know if the senator did this himself. He strikes me as more of a guy who hires out his dirty work." After all, that was exactly what they thought he'd done in D.C.—hired Jack to take out the EOD.

And as far as getting rid of her and Thomas, well, she was sure that counted as dirty work.

"He just tried to kill two federal agents," Thomas's lips brushed against her neck. Had he meant to do that? Surely not. "Whether he did it himself or he hired someone, we're getting the guy. At first light, we're finding a way out of this place, and we're going after him."

First light. That certainly seemed very far away.

"He panicked." That was the only explanation she had. "Something set him off during our meeting." Something they'd said or done.

"He got set off because the FBI was at his door. The guy's probably trying to run as fast and as far as he can right now."

Noelle wasn't so sure. If he thought they were dead, why would he bother to run?

"But I'll find him," Thomas vowed. "I won't stop until I do."

The fire surged a bit higher then, sending sparks into the air.

"We should get some sleep." His voice softened a bit. "Who the hell knows what we'll face tomorrow."

Since they'd just survived one attempt on their lives, Noelle knew he was right.

Her gaze drifted away from the fire. She glanced at the flickering shadows lining the walls. This place… It was just like the cabin that haunted her nightmares. Those nightmares chased her wherever she went, no matter what she did.

"You're too tense," he said. "Look, I get that you don't like me, but—"

"I like you just fine." How awkward was this conversation? But he had a right to know… "It's not you that I'm afraid of, okay? It's… this place."

He was silent behind her. But his fingers moved lightly against her stomach. Almost as if he were caressing her.

"We're safe."

Her gaze slid to the right. His gun was there. Within easy reach. "Sometimes, I don't ever feel safe." As soon as she said the words, Noelle wished she could call them back. She'd never made that confession to anyone.

"Why not?" His hold definitely tightened then.

Noelle shook her head. She was feeling warmer, so much warmer now. The shivers and shudders were easing. "Because I'm never sure what waits in the darkness." But she wasn't talking about the darkness outside the cabin. She was talking about the darkness in her own mind.

He was silent behind her.

And Noelle found she couldn't stop talking, not to him. Not then. "When I was seventeen, I was…taken." Just saying the words hurt, but it also seemed a relief to put them out there. "I was missing from my home for over forty-eight hours before the police found me." She was glad she wasn't looking into his face when she told this story. Noelle wasn't sure she wanted to see his reaction. "Forty-eight hours," she said again, whispering the words. "And to this day, I still can't remember a single thing that happened during that time." When she tried to remember, she only saw the darkness.

"Maybe you're better off not remembering."

That was what her mother had told her, over and over. Her mother had thought it would be better to just move forward. To put those two days into the back of her mind and pretend they hadn't happened.

But they *had* happened. They'd changed her.

"When the police found me, a dead man was in the cabin with me."

Silence. Then, "You think you killed him?"

"I was tied, bound to a chair. Someone else was there." The man's accomplice? Another shudder had her body quaking. But she didn't know if that shudder came from the cold or from the fear in her belly. "A killer was there, and I can't remember a thing about him."

That scared her more than anything else. Because that man—that killer—he could be anyone. He could be anywhere. She could have met him a hundred times and never known.

She'd become a profiler because of what happened. Because she wanted to be able to see the murderers out there. To look behind the masks they wore.

What she'd discovered during the course of her career was that monsters were real. They just wore the guise of men.

Her eyes squeezed closed. She didn't know why she'd revealed so much to Thomas. In the harsh light of dawn, she knew she'd regret sharing so much with him. But, right then, she still just felt that strange relief.

And the fear slid away as the fire warmed her and he held her close. It was odd to feel so secure…in the arms of a dragon.

THE DOOR TO Lawrence Duncan's study opened with a rasp of sound. Lawrence glanced up, expecting to see Paula, but she wasn't in the doorway. Still, he smiled when he saw just who *had* come to pay him a late-night visit. "I take it that you accomplished our task?"

His visitor took a step inside his study. "Their vehicle won't be found."

"Good." His eyes narrowed as he studied the man before him. "This shouldn't have happened, you know. I'm supposed to be clear. Instead, I'm cleaning up your messes." His breath heaved out. "Noelle Evers. She should've died years ago, and we both know it."

The floor creaked as the man edged closer to Lawrence. "I didn't want Noelle to die this way. I wanted—"

"To cut her throat yourself? Yes, well, I know how you enjoy getting up close, but that wasn't going to happen." Lawrence shot to his feet and paced toward the window on the right. When he looked out, he just saw darkness. "She's not some scared kid any longer. She's FBI. And if we hadn't taken her out then—"

His words ended, cut off with a gurgle of sound because—because a knife had just sliced across his throat.

"I was saving her for later." The words were snarled into Lawrence's ear. "She would have been special. Now she's *gone*."

Lawrence's hand flew to his neck, but he couldn't stop the flow. His knees gave way. He tried to grab for the window curtain, but his bloody hands just slipped over the fabric. He hit the floor.

His eyes were open and staring up at the killer above him.

"You were a threat, too," the killer told him. "Because you knew what I'd done." He smiled down at Lawrence. "But you won't tell anyone now, will you? You *can't* tell anyone." His smile faded away. "And I won't be on your leash any longer. From here on out, no one controls me."

SHE WAS ASLEEP in his arms. Noelle's breathing was easy and soft, and all of the tension had drained from her body. She was a silken weight against Thomas, and her scent—light and sweet—wrapped deeply around him.

He'd told her that it wasn't personal. That it was just about survival.

He was such a liar. With her, everything was personal. It had been, for far longer than she realized.

His left arm was still under her head. His fingers were starting to go numb, but Thomas didn't care. She was comfortable, and he had no intention of moving. He'd dreamed of holding her before, but he hadn't ever thought he'd actually get this close to her.

Some dreams were so much better in reality. His lips brushed lightly over her hair. If she'd been awake, he wouldn't have dared such a move. But asleep…

I'll make my control hold. It was a good thing she wasn't aware right then. There'd be no hiding the arousal he felt when she was near.

He figured an hour had passed. The flames were still crackling. They were secure for the night, but he had no intention of closing his eyes anytime soon. With his perfect temptation nestled so closely to him, sleep wasn't exactly high on his priority list. Besides, he wanted to keep her safe, and keeping Noelle safe meant someone had to stay awake for guard duty.

"Let me go…"

The words were so soft that, at first, he thought he'd just imagined them, but then Noelle began to struggle lightly against his hold. "Please," she whispered, and the plea cut right through him. "Don't hurt me."

Never.

She twisted in his hold, her struggles growing stronger. "Let me go!"

"Noelle." He knew she was having a nightmare. She'd revealed so much to him in the darkness. "Noelle, you're safe." With him, she'd always be safe. He wished she would realize that.

She rolled then, and he eased his hold as she turned toward him. Her body came flush against his, and he was stunned to see her eyes were wide open. "Noelle?"

"I won't tell," she said, and her voice was wrong. Too soft. Too lost. "Just let me go." Her hands pushed against him.

He shifted his body, caught her hands and pinned them lightly to the floor. "Look at me." Thomas said the words deliberately because he knew Noelle wasn't seeing him. She was just staring at images from her past.

How often did this happen? How often did she get trapped in the same nightmare?

"Don't hurt me…"

She was breaking him. Thomas had to make Noelle see what was right in front of her. Damn it, he'd worried when he saw this place it might stir up her past, but he hadn't exactly been given a choice. It had been this dump of a cabin or nothing, and he hadn't planned to just stand by while she suffered.

"Noelle…" Her name was a growl of frustration. Then he did the only thing he could—Thomas kissed her.

He'd often thought about kissing Noelle, tasting her. But he'd sure never imagined their first taste would be like this.

Her lips were soft beneath his. He kissed her slowly, carefully. He wanted to pull her back from the past and get her to see the present. To see him.

She stiffened against him as he kissed her. He knew awareness was flooding back for her. He knew he should pull away.

He also knew that he wanted her more than he'd ever wanted any other woman.

So when her lips parted in surprise, he didn't do the right thing. He didn't pull back and ask her if she was okay.

He kissed her harder. He thrust his tongue into her mouth, and he savored her. With every movement of his lips against hers, Thomas just wanted more.

He wanted everything.

One day, he'd get it.

Her breasts were pressed to his chest. Her smooth legs were trapped between his thighs. And—

She was kissing him back. Slowly at first then with more passion, with a need he hadn't expected.

Desire surged within him. *Noelle wants me, too.* He'd never expected to find the passion hiding behind her fear.

His heart thudded in his ears. He was so close to having her. Only the thin scrap of lace she wore shielded her from him. When he'd first seen the black bra and that tiny bit that passed for her panties, lust had surged through him.

He wanted to touch every inch of her then.

He freed her wrists so he could explore her body. He'd make it good for her. He'd give her so much pleasure. Enough to chase away any nightmares that ever dared to whisper through her mind again.

When he let her wrists go, her hands immediately curled around his shoulders. He kissed his way down her throat. Her pulse raced beneath his mouth, and Thomas had to lick that spot right there. She moaned lightly, and his teeth grazed over the flesh. He wanted her so much his whole body seemed to flash molten hot.

"Thomas?" Desire was in her voice, and he loved the sound of his name on her lips.

His hand was on her rib cage. He wanted that bra gone. He wanted—

Her.

"Thomas…no, we're partners." Confusion fought with the desire in Noelle's husky voice. "I— *We can't.*"

Oh, they could. They could do it so well and so long, but Thomas stilled at her words. His head lifted. He met her stare, and he knew she'd read fierce hunger in his eyes.

Her hands seemed to burn against his skin. He was so close to the thing he wanted most. So very close.

Thomas pulled away from her and rose to his feet. His jeans were still a little damp, but he pulled them on. Staying naked with her sure wasn't an option then. He turned his back to her as he yanked up the zipper.

"I…I didn't mean to let things get so far." Her soft voice came from behind him.

He sucked in a deep breath, then glanced over his shoulder at her. She'd sat up and her hands were now curled around her folded knees. Damn. Noelle was the sexiest thing he'd ever seen. "You were having a bad dream."

Her brows rose at that.

"I kissed you to try and wake you up." Only she hadn't been sleeping, not really. He thought maybe she'd had more of a flashback than a nightmare. Thomas cleared his throat. "I'm the one who didn't mean to let things get this far." Not yet. He had plans for Noelle, and those plans hadn't included this pit stop at a rundown shack in the middle of nowhere.

"I don't remember the nightmare." Her gaze dropped from his. "But then, I never do."

He turned to fully face her. The fire crackled behind him. "Maybe it's good to get a few things out in the open now."

Her chin lifted as her eyes found his once more.

"I want you."

"We're partners—"

"It's a temporary assignment, and we both know it. Mercer doesn't plan to keep you in the field. He wants you in the EOD main office, working up your profiles. This is a one-shot mission for us." So the normal rules weren't applying. When it came to Noelle, Thomas had no rules. "I want you," he said again, "and unless I'm mistaken, you want me, too."

She didn't speak.

His jaw locked. He'd felt her desire, tasted it. He knew—

"I do," Noelle said, the words so quiet he had to strain in order to hear them.

His heart seemed to stop at that admission.

"But I know better than to take everything I want. Especially when what I want can be dangerous to me."

"You can trust me," he growled. He wasn't a threat to her. Damn it, yes, he knew the stories that circulated about him at the EOD. That the Dragon was a cold-blooded killer with ice in his veins and that he killed without remorse.

That isn't me. He needed Noelle to see him for the man he truly was.

Her body tensed. "I can't trust myself."

He didn't even know what that meant.

But before he could question her more, he heard the faint roar of—an engine?

He saw Noelle's head whip toward the door, and he knew she'd heard the sound, too. He grabbed for the rest of his clothes and dressed as quickly as he could. Noelle was scrambling to her feet and pulling on her still-wet clothing.

His fingers curled around his gun. Was that a rescuer coming to find them, someone who'd been alerted by the smoke rising from the old chimney? Or was it the maniac in the truck, coming back to finish them off? Thomas had known the fire would pose risks for him and Noelle. The smoke would give away their location, but staying warm had been a priority.

The roar of the approaching engine grew louder.

Noelle hurried to Thomas's side. "Stay behind me," he told her with a firm glare. "Until we find out just who is coming this way."

"You're the one with the gun," she said with a shrug as she lifted her hands. "Letting you take the lead is more than fine by me."

He cracked open the front door. He could see the bright glint of headlights coming toward the cabin. That roar—it was from what looked like a snowplow. Thomas could just make out its bulk.

He inched onto the sagging porch, keeping his gun at his side. A quick count showed him three vehicles were coming his way, and none of those vehicles looked like the truck that had run them off the road. Actually one of those vehicles—

A siren screamed on. Blue lights flashed.

Right. One of those vehicles looked like a deputy's car.

More bright lights flooded the scene, illuminating Thomas and Noelle on the porch. Thomas wisely kept his weapon hidden.

Noelle's arm brushed against Thomas's side. "We're FBI!" Noelle called out as she moved forward. They were both supposed to keep using that cover, no matter what.

Doors slammed. Two men ran toward them. "We were hoping it was you," one of the man huffed out. "I'm Sheriff Glen Hodges. Your FBI boss has been calling our office for hours because you missed some sort of check-in."

Ah, that boss would be Mercer, and yes, they had missed their check-in. Thomas was actually surprised Mercer hadn't sent the National Guard after them. When it came to protecting his agents, Mercer was as fierce as any lion.

"We saw the smoke," the man beside Sheriff Hodges said, as he rocked forward onto the balls of his feet. "No one has been using Brian Lakely's place in years, so we thought it might be you."

Thomas advanced toward the men.

"Did you have car trouble?" Hodges asked, shaking his head. "How the heck did you wind up out here?"

"We had car trouble," Thomas agreed softly. "And the trouble started when some bozo ran us off the road and left us for dead."

"What?" The shocked exclamation came as the sheriff shot back a good two feet. "But we don't have trouble like that out here in Camden—"

"Well," Thomas drawled, "it looks like you do now. Because someone out there just tried to kill two federal agents." Thomas planned to get his hands on that *someone* very soon.

Senator Duncan, I'm coming for you.

Chapter Three

"Uh, are you real sure you want to do this?" Sheriff Hodges asked as he slammed his car door and turned toward Noelle and Thomas. The snow was still falling.

They were outside the senator's home. She and Thomas had insisted they be brought straight over. Noelle wanted to look into the senator's eyes and *see* his reaction to their survival. If he was the guy who'd just tried to send them to an icy grave, his reaction would tell her everything she needed to know.

"Senator Duncan..." The sheriff's voice was cautious. "He has a lot of power around here."

"We're not worried about his power." Noelle brushed past the sheriff and headed for the gate that led to the senator's property. It was ajar, so she just kept marching right up to the front door. She was wearing a thick coat about two sizes too big, a spare that Hodges kept in his trunk. Gloves covered her fingers, and a big woolen cap swallowed her hair. Thomas followed right on her heels. After what they'd been through, there was no way they'd allow the senator to slip through their fingers that night.

"Maybe you two should go to the local doc's place," the sheriff said as he rushed after them. "Make sure you're not suffering from some kind of trauma."

Noelle wasn't concerned about trauma. Before she could slam her fist against the door, Thomas beat her to it. He pounded hard enough to shake the façade.

Lights flooded on from the interior of the house.

"I'm gonna be in so much trouble," Hodges muttered.

The man needed to grow a backbone.

Eyes narrowed, Noelle focused on the door. When it swung open a few minutes later, a disheveled Paula Quill stood in the doorway.

"Agents?" Paula shoved back her hair. "What are you doing here?"

Noelle advanced and Paula fell back. Noelle figured that counted as an invitation to enter the place. "We're here to see the senator, *now.*"

"But it's the middle of the night!" Paula's hands tightly gripped the front of her robe. "You can't just barge in here—"

That was exactly what they'd just done.

Noelle glanced to the left and saw a light was on in the senator's study, and its door was slightly open. Just like the gate. The senator should really watch that tendency to keep inviting folks in.

"The senator is *sleeping*," Paula snapped as she moved to stand directly in front of Noelle. "You'll have to come back in the morning if you want another appointment with him."

Noelle simply walked around the other woman and headed for the study.

"Sorry, ma'am," Thomas murmured to Paula, "but this appointment can't wait."

Noelle's steps quickened as she approached that study door. Thomas was close. She could hear him following her. "Senator Duncan," Noelle called, raising her voice, "I hope you—" She fully pushed open the door, and her words broke off.

Noelle didn't see the senator in the office. He wasn't at his desk.

"I *told* you," Paula said, voice tight. "He's asleep. He's upstairs! Now, leave."

But…Noelle could smell something in that room. A familiar, gut-tightening scent. Instead of leaving, she advanced. Every muscle in her body tightened.

She glanced over her shoulder and saw

Thomas's eyes were narrowed and currently sweeping over the room.

She looked behind the desk. Looked behind the leather couch…

And saw the body.

"That's not sleeping," Thomas said flatly as he peered down at the senator. "That's dead."

Paula ran toward the sofa. When she saw Duncan, Paula screamed.

"Our chief suspect is dead."

Noelle glanced over when Thomas made this grim announcement. They were at the sheriff's station in Camden, in fresh clothes, and the two of them were currently heading the investigation into the senator's death. When they'd found the body, Sheriff Hodges had pretty much gone into shock.

"Things like this just don't happen in Camden…" Those had been the sheriff's hushed words once Paula Quill finally stopped screaming. It had taken at least fifteen minutes to calm down that woman.

To Noelle, it appeared as if the quiet town of Camden was having one hell of a night.

"Yeah, Mercer, I'm sure the guy in the truck wanted us dead. It was no mere hit-and-run. We were targeted." Thomas turned toward Noelle as he kept the phone to his ear. "My money was on the senator being behind that attack, but with him dead…" Thomas exhaled. "I'm not sure what's going on now."

Neither was Noelle.

"Right," Thomas said into the phone as his shoulders straightened. "We'll keep the FBI cover, and we'll report back on everything we find." He ended the call and tossed his phone onto the nearby desk.

They'd taken over one of the empty offices at the sheriff's station so they could have some privacy—and a base for their operations.

"Mercer wants us to stay here until we find the killer." Thomas ran a hand through his hair. "Our FBI cover positions us to lead the case, so he thinks we can control the investigation."

They could. If Sheriff Hodges called to verify their credentials, Noelle knew Mercer would just pull strings to make sure that verification went through without a hitch.

"Tell me what's happening," Thomas said as he crossed his arms over his chest and studied her. "You're the one who knows killers so well."

Yes, she did. Noelle cleared her throat. "The senator knew his killer. There was no sign of a struggle, and since none of the alarms were triggered in the house, I'm thinking Duncan even let the guy inside." A bad mistake. He'd trusted the wrong person. "There were no hesitation wounds on the senator's body. The knife sliced straight across his carotid artery. The senator...he would've been dead in moments." With his throat cut, the man hadn't been able to cry out for help. He'd just been able to die.

Noelle forced herself to take a long, deep breath. "I think we're looking for a man who has killed before." If it had been the killer's first time, the attack would've been more disorganized. Senator Duncan might have even been able to fight back. "And knife attacks...they're more personal. Using a knife is a type of intimate kill for many perpetrators."

His golden eyes gleamed. "So you think the man we're looking for was a friend of Duncan's."

"Friend, relative, maybe even an employee. He was someone who had access to the senator. Someone who could come to his house late at night and expect a meeting." She wasn't going to ignore the obvious. "I can think of one main reason for a meeting that late."

Thomas nodded. "A meeting that probably occurred right after our *accident* on the bridge." His hands dropped back to his sides.

Yes, they had both heard the M.E. reveal the estimated time of death.

"We already suspected that the senator didn't like to get up close with his dirty work. He sent someone in D.C. to attack Mercer, so maybe he sent someone to take care of us, too." She licked her lips. "Only that *someone* turned on the senator." *Why?* It was her job to find out why. Her job to understand the killers. Their motivations. Their darkness.

"You think we're looking at a professional."

"Of a sort, yes."

"So…" Thomas cocked his head to the right as he studied her. "What will this professional do when he realizes that he didn't succeed in taking us out? *If,* of course, he was the one who came after us."

Well, that was easy enough to answer. "There are two choices. He'll just cut his losses and get out of town or he'll try to finish the job."

Thomas's lips curved into a chilling smile. "I'd like to see him try."

His hands were shaking.

The killer glanced down at them. They were trembling again. And even though he'd thrown away his bloodstained gloves, he could swear he saw red on his fingertips.

Duncan's gone.

It felt so good to be free of the jerk. Duncan had always been controlling him…warning him.

No more.

The sun had risen. The snow had finally stopped falling. It was *his* day. No more taking orders. No more hiding.

He'd do what he wanted.

The FBI agents were gone. *She* was gone.

And the senator's body would be found at any time.

He was free.

The sound of laughter drifted on the wind. The light, musical sound caught his attention. He glanced over at the diner on the right. It had just opened for breakfast. He watched as a young girl—looked as though she was barely sixteen—tried to push back the drift in front of the entrance. She was laughing because the snow kept falling back on her. Her red hair glinted in the light.

He stared at her, remembering the past.

She was so busy at her job she didn't even see him. The road was empty. The diner always opened first thing. It would be a while before any locals wandered into the place.

He started walking toward her. She didn't even look up as he approached. He could see her name tag.

Jenny.

Jenny must be new at the diner. He'd never seen her there before.

Then he was just a few feet from Jenny.

Her hair was a deep, dark red. She'd braided it and the braid hung over her shoulder. He was so close to her. Close enough to touch.

Jenny looked up then, and she gasped when she saw him. A hand rose to her chest, and the shovel slipped from her fingers.

He smiled at her. "Morning, ma'am."

She blinked, and some of the alarm faded from her gaze. That was good. That was real good. He didn't want her scared. Not yet.

He drew even closer to her. Close enough to catch her scent. She smelled sweet. He liked that. His gaze slid toward the diner. The shades were still pulled. He couldn't see in. That meant no one could see out.

"We'll be open in about ten more minutes," Jenny told him. "The cook's getting things going now."

The cook. That would be the big, ex-lumberjack named Henry. But if Henry was getting things going in the kitchen...

Then he can't see us out here.

And Jenny was so perfect. She reminded him of what he'd lost.

His hand lifted and brushed over her cheek.

Her eyes widened as she sucked in a sharp breath. "Mister—"

"It will hurt, Jenny," he warned her.

Too late, Jenny opened her mouth to scream. She never had the chance to make a sound.

NOELLE WAS ABOUT to fall flat on her face. It took all of the energy she had to climb the steps leading up to their cabin.

This place wasn't like the one-room shack they'd slept in before. This cabin was more like a luxury resort and as far from the place in her nightmares as possible.

The EOD was footing the bill for these digs, so Noelle was more than happy to escape to the fine lodgings.

She'd been up for over thirty-six hours, minus that one rough hour of sleep she'd gotten while she'd been in Thomas's arms.

Her gaze slanted toward him. *I want you, and unless I'm mistaken, you want me, too.* His words kept echoing through her mind.

The problem was Noelle wasn't used to taking what she wanted. She was used to closing herself off from others. Used to waking from dark dreams she could never fully remember—alone.

"We need to head back to the sheriff's station at eighteen hundred hours," Thomas said as he secured the front door behind them. He glanced around the cabin. A spiral staircase led upstairs. "That gives us a few hours to sleep."

And sleep was certainly her priority because of the whole almost-falling-on-her-face bit, but...

She kept thinking about what it had been like to be held in his arms. To kiss him. To touch him.

His head cocked as his eye raked over her. "Something wrong?"

"I'm just...trying to figure out who could've killed the senator." Well, she should be doing that, anyway.

He grunted as he headed toward her. "Mercer is arranging for new clothes to be delivered to us."

Since their bags were at the bottom of an icy lake, she appreciated the arrangement.

"Get some sleep, get some food, and then you'll be able to work up a profile."

He sure sounded confident. But it wasn't as if she just waved a wand and magically figured out a killer. "I'll need to head back to Lawrence's place. I want to search every inch of that house."

He flashed her a hard smile. "Already on the to-do list. Mercer wants us to find evidence proving Lawrence is our guy—and if the senator was working with anyone else in the attack against the EOD, we need to find out just who that person is."

Right. Because the case wasn't closed, not even with the death of their chief suspect.

"There are supposed to be two bedrooms upstairs," Thomas added as he glanced up at the winding staircase. "Pick which one you want, and I'll take the other."

I'll take the one with you.

Wait, no. She had *not* nearly said that. She must be more exhausted than she'd realized. Noelle turned on her heel and hurried toward the stairs.

"Do you need to talk?"

Her hand curled around the bannister. His voice had been so rough. "About what?"

"About the nightmares you have."

How could she talk about what she didn't remember?

"You begged someone not to hurt you. Pleaded for them to let you go." The hardwood floor creaked beneath his footsteps. "And you promised not to tell…"

She glanced over her shoulder at him. "I don't remember any of that." Her heart raced in her chest.

"You do when you let down your guard. When you sleep, that veil in your mind falls away."

She shook her head. "I… No, you're wrong."

He was just a few feet away. "Have you

ever thought that maybe you just don't want to remember?"

The dead man on the floor...the blood on her hands...

"I want to remember." Those forty-eight hours had shattered her life. Her mother had wanted to push them away while Noelle had desperately wanted to grab that time back.

His gaze held hers. "There are plenty of moments from my life that I wish I could forget."

She thought of the scars on his body. His captivity. "What if you had the scars, but no memory of how you'd gotten them?" She didn't have scars on her body. Not on the outside, anyway. But those two nights had left deep marks inside of her. "Every time you looked at them, wouldn't you wonder?"

He took another gliding step toward her. She tilted back her head to keep meeting his gaze.

"When I look at the scars I have now," Thomas said, "I remember how much my captors enjoyed cutting into me. They wanted me to break." His eyes narrowed. "I didn't. No matter what they did to me, I didn't break."

No, the Dragon hadn't. But had she? In those lost hours, what had Noelle done?

"Then I remember what it was like to kill them." His hands fisted. "You know what I am and what I've done. But when I close my eyes, I don't like seeing the bodies in my mind."

You know what I am. She reached out to him and pressed her hand to his clenched fist. "You're a soldier. You survived. You fought. *That's what you did.*"

His gaze fell to her hand. Her skin was so pale while his was a dark tan.

"You need to be careful," Thomas warned her. His stare was still focused on her hand.

"Careful?"

"You already know I want you, and right now...my control isn't real strong."

She pulled back. "I didn't mean—"

A muscle jerked in his jaw. "I know what you meant, but I'm running on no sleep and the memory of you being nearly naked in my arms. So you should go to your room, I'll go to mine, and when we wake up in a few hours, we can just pretend we never crossed the line between us."

The line between partners...and lovers?

"I'll stay hands-off, and we'll keep things just business." The gold in his eyes heated. "And we'll get the job done here so we can head back to D.C."

That was the right thing to do. They had to work together. But... *I want him.*

Noelle turned away. She climbed up the

stairs. She was right at the top when she just had to look back once more.

He was still standing at the base. That hot, golden gaze was focused on her.

"When did we meet before?" Noelle asked quietly.

A mask seemed to slip over his face.

"Don't lie to me." So, maybe she was also running on no sleep and the memory of him being so warm and naked beside her. Because she sure felt as if she'd been pushed to the edge. "You're familiar to me. And sometimes, sometimes…like right *now,* I'll catch you looking at me as if—as if you know me."

"I do know you," he growled. "We're working together and—"

"You knew me before the EOD. You even slipped up once." Another day, another case, but the words had nagged at her. "You told me that you'd seen me, but I hadn't seen you."

He glanced away from her, giving Noelle his profile. "You don't have clearance to know about all the cases I've worked. So all I can say is that our paths have crossed."

There was more. "Do you always keep secrets from women you want to have sex with?"

His shoulders stiffened. "I keep secrets from everyone." He turned on his heel, giving her his broad back. "Get some sleep. Eighteen hundred hours will be here before you know it."

Frustration had her muscles knotting, but she spun around and pretty much stomped her way into the room at the top of the stairs. The room was filled with heavy oak furniture, and a big, wide picture window overlooked the snow-covered land around the cabin.

The bed was a massive four-poster, which waited in the middle of the room. Noelle stared down at the covers, then she just let herself fall, face-first, into them.

She wanted sleep to take her away because the look in Thomas's gaze... It had unnerved her far too much.

THERE WERE NO creaks from upstairs. No soft rustles of clothing. Noelle had been up there for fifteen minutes, and Thomas was pretty sure the woman had crashed.

He pulled out his phone and called Mercer. The situation was about to slide out of his control, and he needed to know what to do when—

"Don't tell me you've found another body," Mercer said, his words rumbling as the EOD Director answered the call on the second ring.

Thomas's gaze stayed locked on the staircase. "Pairing me with Noelle was a mistake."

Silence.

"She wants me to tell her how I know her." He hated looking right into her eyes and lying. The lies were cutting him up inside.

"You're in Alaska to track down the man who hired the Jack of Hearts to kill me...and to destroy the EOD."

"Yeah, well..." His hand raked through his hair. "All signs indicate that guy is on a slab in the county morgue right now. We'll do recon work after we've had a little time to rest, but Noelle is pushing, and I want to know just how much—"

"You can reveal?" Mercer's tone was measured.

"It's been fifteen years. She still has nightmares."

"I thought she might." It almost sounded as if sympathy was in Mercer's voice. Obviously, they had a bad connection. Mercer felt sympathy for no one. "And that's why she's paired up with you."

"I'm not following you."

"If anyone can help her to remember, it's you. After all, you were there, right?"

He swallowed. "You put us together—because you thought she'd remember me?"

"Well, I'd hoped Noelle would remember you the first time she saw you at the EOD. Maybe get a flashback. Something. That didn't happen, so I figured we needed to step up the game."

Only Mercer thought playing with someone's life constituted a game.

"She's not a victim anymore, she's an agent." Mercer's voice hardened. "Fifteen years ago, we had to protect your cover. You had to vanish from the scene."

But he'd left her behind, and she'd been... shattered.

"Come now, Agent Anthony, I know you've seen her since then. You've watched over her all these years."

Damn it. Mercer and his all-knowing intel. "What I do on my *own* time is none of your—"

"You should be thanking me. I mean, at least you don't have to sneak off to check up on your profiler on your rare off days. Now you get to be up close with her, 24/7."

This was insane. "She doesn't *remember* me."

"She will." Flat. "I think it's possible that Noelle will discover a whole lot while she's in Alaska." A pause. "I want her to rip apart Senator Lawrence Duncan's life. She's just the woman for this job."

Thomas's brows pulled together. "Have you told me everything about this mission?"

"Oh, son, I never tell anyone...everything."

Hell.

"I know you'll guard Dr. Evers. That's your job right now. To make sure that nothing happens to her while she's in Alaska. If I'm going to get to the bottom of this mystery, I need her."

So, Noelle was the brains while Thomas was the killing power. He'd always been a weapon, of one kind or another. From the time he'd turned eighteen...

I have my memories, and sometimes, I hate them. "I'll keep Noelle safe."

"Of course, you will." Now Mercer sounded certain. Almost smug. "It's what you've been doing for the past fifteen years, isn't it?"

Mercer *had* been watching. Far too much.

"Even when she became an FBI agent, you couldn't let go. You thought she still needed you."

No, Mercer had that part all wrong. It wasn't about what Noelle needed.

I need her.

There was so much death in his life. Everywhere he turned. But Noelle, she was the one bright light in the darkness that always seemed to surrounded him.

"This time, she does need you," Mercer's voice held an edge. "So stay close, no matter what happens."

Thomas ended the call. He took his time

climbing those stairs. When he got to the top, he saw the door to Noelle's room had been left ajar.

His fingers pressed against it, opening it just a few more inches. Noelle was on the bed. Her thick hair was a curtain, spilling down her back.

Would nightmares come to her again?

If they did, Thomas hoped she would come to *him*.

Chapter Four

Senator Lawrence Duncan had believed in sur-
rounding himself with the finer things in life.

Noelle put her hands on her hips as she studied the senator's closet. The massive closet was
easily the size of her D.C. bedroom *and* living
room and filled with designer clothing.

"He was ex-navy," Thomas said. "This place
sure is a long way from his life on the ship."

She knew all about Lawrence Duncan's
background. He'd grown up poor in Camden,
Alaska. He joined the navy when he was eighteen. He'd been an enlisted man for eight years,
and when he'd gotten out of the service, the
guy had seemed to skyrocket to power over-
night. He'd come out of the military with some
incredible connections, or else he'd obtained
some very deadly secrets during his time in
the service.

"He was married twice," Noelle murmured
as she studied the closet. Each item was per-

fectly in place. "Both women left him citing ir-
reconcilable differences." But she'd interviewed
those ladies before coming to Camden. Fear
had flashed in their eyes when they spoke of
their husband.

Dominating. Controlling. Their voices had
become whispers when they talked about the
senator.

"He was sleeping with his assistant." Thomas
propped his shoulder against the bedroom wall.

"Her and plenty of other aides." She turned
away from the closet. She'd searched in there,
twice, and found nothing of any real value.
But…something *had* to be in the house. This
place was Lawrence's sanctuary. After he'd left
the navy, he could have started over any place.
But he'd returned to Camden. He'd torn down
his old house and had this mansion built right
in the same spot.

She and Thomas had already confiscated all
of the senator's computer equipment. An ini-
tial search of the material hadn't shed any ad-
ditional light on the attack in D.C.—*or* on the
senator's death—but they had specialists back
at the EOD who'd tear that equipment apart. If
there was intel to find there, they would.

She went toward the window on the left. Looking down, she saw the slumping roof of what

looked like an old shed behind the main house. About fifty yards back, right at the tree line.

The shed made her curious. "He replaced everything else." No, not just replaced. He'd *destroyed* everything else on that property. "Why not that shed? Why is it still out there?"

Before Thomas could answer her, Noelle turned and hurried from the room. Sheriff Hodges glanced up when she rushed down the stairs. His hand was on Paula's shoulder, as if he'd been comforting the woman. Paula's eyes were watering, and her nose was red.

"I should have heard him. I should have helped him!"

Noelle didn't slow to help console the other woman. She figured Hodges had things covered. She made her way to the back of the house and threw open the rear door. The icy air hit her, seeming to chill straight to her bones.

Thomas was behind her. Not speaking but following closely. When they got to the old shed, she saw a big wooden board had been positioned to block the entrance. She grabbed for the board, but Thomas was there, and he heaved it aside.

She pushed open the shed's door. But it really wasn't so much a shed. It reminded her more of an old barn.

The roof was high, there was no floor, just what looked like dirt and straw and—

A trunk sat, half-hidden beneath some old blankets, positioned against the far back wall. Her steps quickened as she approached it.

"Why are we out here, Noelle?" Thomas asked her.

"Because I need to understand Lawrence. He came back here to this exact spot to start his new life, for a reason." She dropped to her knees and pushed aside the blankets that covered the trunk. Then she saw the padlock. The trunk was old and weathered from time, but the padlock was shiny. New.

"If the senator had something valuable, he wouldn't leave it out here." Thomas's words were clipped. "That's probably just some kind of equipment in there he used on his land. He didn't want it stolen so—"

She'd spotted a hammer hanging on a nearby shelf. Noelle grabbed it and started pounding at the lock.

"*Noelle!* Hell, wait, we can get the sheriff to—"

The lock broke. Noelle shoved it aside. She wasn't even sure what she'd expected to find but—

Photographs.

There were dozens of photographs inside the

trunk. The old, Polaroid type. The white edges surrounded the images.

Her fingers were shaking when she reached for the first one. The light from her flashlight bobbed as she tried to focus in on that photo.

A photo of a young girl, a teen, blindfolded, tied to a chair.

A girl with red hair.

The print fell from her fingers, but then Noelle dove forward. Her light shined on all of those snapshots.

Red-haired girls. Teens. Bound. Blindfolded.

"Noelle!" Thomas's fingers curled around her, and he yanked her to her feet.

But it was too late. Because she'd just found another photograph, only this photograph was familiar.

"That's me," she whispered as she stared down at her picture.

Like the other girls, she was blindfolded and tied to a chair.

That image… Dear God, had been taken fifteen years ago, during the two lost days of her life.

"There are ten different girls in these pictures." No emotion entered Noelle's voice, and it was that complete lack of emotion that worried Thomas the most.

They were back at the sheriff's station. It was long past midnight, and Noelle—she'd pinned all of the photos to the wall in their makeshift office. Those images had already been faxed to the EOD. But…

"Are you okay?"

She flinched at the question, and instead of answering, she said, "They're all about the same age. Sixteen or seventeen, females, with red hair—"

His fingers curled around her shoulders and he turned her, forcing her to face him. "Are. You. Okay?"

Her pupils were too big. Her face too pale.

"We have to operate under the assumption the photos are—are trophies that Senator Lawrence kept close because he wanted to relive the abductions—"

"Noelle, you're in the damn photo!"

Her gaze fell to his throat. He saw her swallow. "We always knew that a second man had to be involved in my abduction." Her voice still had no emotion. "I was tied up, so I couldn't have been the one to kill him. Someone else was there the whole time." Slowly, her lashes lifted. "It's possible Senator Lawrence was that someone."

No, it wasn't.

"This is the first lead I've ever had." Her lower lip trembled, but she caught it between her teeth. After a moment, Noelle said, "This is *my* life, and the man who could've told me the truth is dead."

Thomas wasn't exactly mourning the guy.

She pulled in a deep breath. "The EOD is searching Missing Persons databases now, using image-recognition software, but this— this isn't the usual type of case for Mercer's team."

No, it wasn't.

"The FBI should be investigating, and Sheriff Hodges, he *thinks* he's got the FBI." She shook her head. "We have to call them in. The real FBI. If any of those girls are still alive—"

"Do you think they are?"

Because he was watching her so closely, Thomas saw her eyelids flicker.

No, she doesn't.

"Tell me why killers keep trophies," Thomas demanded. Because, yes, he knew exactly what those images were.

"To remind them of the crimes."

"Cadaver dogs are on the way." He'd been pulling some strings of his own while she worked to identify the victims. "There might be more than just photographs buried in that old shed." There had been no floor there. Just earth...

A graveyard? Maybe. He'd be finding out soon.

"I got away." Her voice was a thin whisper. "Maybe some of them did, too. If there's another survivor, if we can find her, then we can figure out how the senator fits into all of this."

Provided Mercer didn't yank them off the case. Because Noelle had been right about the EOD not handling missing-persons cases, and with a potential serial killer involved— Hell, no, this wasn't business as usual for them.

Thomas was used to facing terrorists, arms dealers, but this... This was beyond his realm.

But it was exactly where Noelle thrived.

She'd turned back to study the photographs. "He used a Polaroid so that he wouldn't have to develop his film." Her fingers hovered over the image of herself. "Technology wasn't so advanced back then, he couldn't just snap a picture with his phone, and he wouldn't have wanted anyone to know what he was doing."

"It's possible that all of those images are from at least fifteen years ago."

She nodded. "But a killer like that, he wouldn't just...stop." Softer, she added, "He couldn't. The compulsion to kill would be too strong."

This whole situation wasn't making sense to Thomas. "The guy was a senator. You don't get much more of a high profile. He had guards, reporters, hell, nearly *everyone* dogging his steps. Wouldn't someone have noticed if the guy was abducting girls?"

The image of Lawrence Duncan as a serial killer just wasn't fitting for him.

"He was a hunter." Noelle was still looking at the snapshots. "Maybe he just found something that he really enjoyed hunting. Something…or someone."

Thomas stiffened at her words as memories flooded through his mind. A forest. Darkness. A girl's scream.

Damn it, he *had* to tell her. Mercer could fire him; Thomas didn't care. The photographs changed everything. *We always thought it was just her.*

But it was now obvious Noelle hadn't been the only victim.

"There's something you need to know," Thomas told her, aware his voice had come out a bit rough.

She didn't glance his way.

"Noelle, *look* at me."

Her body turned. Her gaze found his.

"You were right," he said. He didn't know how she was going to react, and in that moment, fear crouched beneath his skin. "We met before you came to work at the EOD."

She stepped toward him as her brows rose. "When?"

"Years ago." He exhaled once more. "It wasn't for long, just an hour, maybe two." Two hours that changed his life and hers.

"Thomas?"

"The first time I saw you...you were running, in the woods..."

Surprise flashed over face. "What are you talking about?"

"You screamed for me to help you."

Her body trembled. The little bit of color in her face drained away. He lunged toward her, worried she might be about to pass out. He grabbed her, holding her tightly. *"Noelle?"*

Her hands twisted so that she was holding him, too. "Why are you saying this? Why are you—?"

The door behind Thomas flew open and crashed into the wall. "I need you two!" Sheriff Hodges yelled. "In the bull pen, *now!*"

That man had the worst timing in the world. Thomas threw a glare over his shoulder, and he didn't care if the sheriff saw him basically embracing Noelle right then. "We're busy. It's just gonna have to wait—"

"The hell it is." Red stained the sheriff's

cheeks as he pointed to the pictures on the wall. "I just got a report of a missing girl. A girl who looks just like those others pinned up there."

Then Thomas heard it. The soft sound of... sobbing? Coming from outside the room.

"Jenny Tucker has been missing since around six this morning," Hodges told them. "We don't... *Things like this don't happen in Camden.*"

Noelle shoved past the sheriff as she made her way to the door. "Yes, they do."

She yanked open the door and hurried out of the office. Thomas spared a hard glance for the sheriff. Hodges appeared to have aged about ten years. The lines near his eyes and mouth were deeper, and the sheriff's shoulders slumped. "I don't... I don't know what to do. I arrest a few drunks every now and then." He swallowed, and his Adam's apple bobbed. "You've got to help us, Agent Anthony. This isn't what I do."

It wasn't what Thomas did, either. He was used to going right after a target and taking out his prey. Not playing a cat-and-mouse game with a serial killer.

He turned on his heel and followed after Noelle. She'd stopped beside a woman with short, red hair. The woman was huddled in a chair, and tears streamed down her cheeks.

"I—I thought she was working late.... I kept

waiting for my Jenny to come h-home...." Her body shuddered. "It was... It was her first day. She was gonna work weekends at the diner."

Noelle patted the woman's shoulder.

"Sh-she never came home."

The floor creaked behind Thomas.

"Jenny's like the girls in all those pictures," the sheriff said, his voice low and carrying only to Thomas's ears. "Is she...is she already dead?"

"I don't know." His hands had fisted at his sides. "It's too early to know anything. The girl could've run off with a boyfriend. She could be at a friend's house. We can't make any conclusions yet." But his gut was tight, and he couldn't help remembering another long-ago night. One that had been filled with the sound of screams...and the red of blood.

THE SMALL CABIN was perfect. Isolated. Secure.

He'd lit a lantern so he could see the girl. She was bound, blindfolded and shivering from the cold.

She hadn't talked much. But then, with a gag in her mouth, talking wouldn't be easy. When she'd woken up, she'd cried for her mother, but he'd stopped those cries easily enough with the gag.

He stared down at her. She was slumped in

the chair. Just watching her brought back so many memories for him.

He'd been a different man back then.

Unfocused. So eager for the cries…

Everything had changed for him, though. In one night. With one kill.

Everything.

He couldn't go back to being the same man. The spike of adrenaline in his blood—it just wasn't the same with the girls any longer. He didn't feel the rush. The thrill.

His hand tightened around the knife in his hand. There wasn't any challenge with little Jenny. Once, there had been. No more.

He was used to bigger game now.

He turned from the girl. He needed to head into town for a while. Had Duncan's body been found? He needed to make sure his bases were covered, and he needed to line up a new job. After he killed Jenny, he'd have to leave the area for good.

It was time to move on.

Camden was a wasteland. Ice and snow. Next time, he'd try someplace warmer.

Maybe he'd head back to Alabama. Or Florida. The memories there were so much damn better.

"WE HAVE TO call in the FBI." Noelle turned toward Thomas as soon as he cut off the engine of their rental car. It was another SUV, which the sheriff had gotten for them. They were parked just a few feet away from the entrance of the only diner in Camden—the presumed spot of Jenny Tucker's abduction. Noelle had known she had to get out here to investigate for herself, but that investigation just wasn't going to be good enough.

Thomas frowned at her. "As far as the locals are concerned, we *are* the FBI."

She shook her head. "The EOD doesn't investigate abductions like this. You *know* that."

Hostage retrieval. Unconventional warfare. Target destruction. She knew the key words for missions the EOD agents took. But this case...

My past.

It was different.

"Mercer will pull us off the investigation as soon as he finds out what's happening. And we can't just leave the girl out there. We *have* to call in the FBI." She had friends at the FBI who should be working this case. If she put in just a fast call to them, those special agents would be on the first flight out there.

But does Jenny have that long?

"I figure that I'm staring at Jenny Tucker's best hope of survival," Thomas said flatly as his gaze held hers. "Mercer told me that you were the best profiler he'd ever seen. If anyone can catch the guy out there, I think it would be you."

But Thomas didn't get it. She shoved back the hair that had fallen over her forehead. "My mind… It's all messed up." Her voice thickened and she tried to swallow the lump in her throat as Thomas watched her with that deep, golden gaze. "Every time I try to think about Jenny or the man who took her, I just see my own picture, pinned to the wall at the station."

Her past. The secrets she'd sought for so long—they were all tangled up in what was happening in Camden.

Her breath seemed to burn her lungs. "I don't have the distance needed for this case. It's too personal." She couldn't separate her own feelings from what was happening. Jenny… *Jenny could be me.* Only Noelle had gotten lucky. She'd been rescued.

Jenny hadn't.

"I don't think distance is what this case needs." His words were a deep rumble as his finger slid over the steering wheel. "I think you're what that girl out there needs. If she really was taken, then you know exactly what that is like."

No, she didn't. Because she couldn't remember anything about her abduction.

He hesitated a moment as he studied her,

then he slowly inclined his head. "But I'll talk to the boss, if that's what you want. We'll get other FBI agents down here."

"Thank you," she whispered.

"But *you* need to stay on point. We both do. We can't blow our cover, because I think this is about a whole lot more than one girl's abduction. The senator was murdered, and we still need to figure out how he fits into this mess."

Yes, they did.

Noelle turned from him and pushed against the handle of her door. His hand flew out, stopping her before she could leave the vehicle. "You're not alone in this, understand? Whatever happens, whatever we discover, I'm going to be right by your side."

She nodded. "Because you're my partner." She'd learned that about the EOD. A partner always had your back. A partner would protect you to the bitter end, a partner would—

"No, that's not why." His fingers lifted and curled around her chin. That golden gaze of his heated even more. She saw the need in his eyes. Her heart raced faster. "You can count on me."

She had to look away from that deep stare because Noelle was afraid Thomas would see too much in her own eyes. She'd been alone for so long. But he was offering her something else. Something she was afraid to take.

She pushed open her car door and the cold air rushed against her skin. The lights from the diner were on, glowing brightly even though it was close to ten o'clock.

Noelle stared at the area around the diner. A few old buildings, which were boarded up. A lone road, which stretched away and disappeared into the darkness.

Camden wasn't a thriving town, she had read during her pretrip research. It had lost most of its residents as the younger generation moved off to bigger cities. Because the businesses were vanishing and the people were leaving, there just hadn't been anyone out there to see Jenny.

Before they'd left the station, the sheriff had checked in with all of Jenny's friends. No one had seen the girl, and the friends had all claimed Jenny had no boyfriend. They'd been adamant she *couldn't* have run off with someone.

The snow crunched beneath Noelle's feet. She saw the open sign on the diner's door. A man, tall, with dark hair, was inside and heading toward the front.

Thomas was at Noelle's side. He grabbed for

the handle and pulled open the door. The bell overhead gave a light jingle of sound.

"Sorry," the man inside rasped. "We're closing."

Noelle pulled out her ID. "Henry Price?" The sheriff had given her the guy's name.

The man nodded as his gaze jerked down to her ID.

"I'm Agent Noelle Evers, and this is my partner, Agent Thomas Anthony. We need to ask you some questions about Jenny."

Henry rubbed a hand over his bleary eyes. "Already talked to the sheriff on the phone."

"And now you're going to talk with us," Thomas said simply. The bell jingled again as the door closed behind them.

Henry shook his head. "I don't know anything. The girl was here this morning. I told her to go and clear the snow from the front, but instead of doing her job..." He turned away and headed for the kitchen. "She just left. You try to help some people, and they just turn on you—"

"Mr. Price." Anger snapped in Noelle's words.

Henry stopped and glanced back at her. A frown pulled down his brows.

"I don't know what you *think* is happening here," Noelle told him, her voice tight with barely held fury, "but Jenny Tucker's mother is down at the sheriff's station right now, her heart breaking because she believes that her daughter was abducted."

He waved his hand. "She's a teenager. They're always trying to cut out of this town and find some adventure."

"None of her friends believe that she cut out of town. And…other evidence…we have suggests that Jenny could be the potential target of a kidnapper in the area." She wouldn't tell him about Jenny matching the physical description of the other victims. They still didn't know what had become of those victims.

Henry blinked as what could have been worry flashed in his eyes. "I didn't hear anything. I mean, if someone took her, she would've screamed right?"

"Not if she didn't have the chance." Thomas's voice was cold.

Henry's gaze flew to the door. "The shovel was outside. When I went looking for her, it was propped right on the side of the building. Like she'd just gotten bored, left it there and walked away."

Thomas took a step forward. "We're going to need that shovel."

They'd dust it for prints. Maybe they'd get lucky. If the girl's abductor had touched it with his bare fingers and the guy was in the system, they could get a hit on his identity.

Henry nodded. "Yeah, yeah…" He turned away once more.

Noelle grabbed his arm. "I need you to think very hard for me. When you went outside and you saw that shovel, did you notice anything else?" Snow had fallen since this morning. By now, it would've covered any signs left behind by Jenny and her abductor.

Henry frowned down at her hand. "I don't… I don't think so."

"Were there footprints in the snow?" she pressed. "Any vehicles that didn't belong?"

His eyes narrowed as he glanced back up at her face. "I think I saw one set of footprints leading toward the parking lot. That's why I thought it was just Jenny leaving."

One set. Which would imply Jenny *had* left on her own. Or else her abductor had carried her off.

"You have any customers here who seem particularly interested in girls around Jenny's age?" This question came from Thomas.

Henry blanched. "No, man, just…*no*."

Noelle dropped her hold on him. She wanted to get outside and take a look around that parking lot. "If you think of anything else, let us know."

"I'll get the shovel."

"*I'll* get it," Thomas said. "We don't want to destroy any evidence that might be left on it."

"I used it all day," Henry said as he hurried down the narrow aisle that led to the kitchen. "I didn't think... I used it *all damn day.*"

Noelle turned away from the men. Her gaze fixed on the diner's windows. If Henry had been working in the kitchen when Jenny was taken, no, he wouldn't have been able to see anything at all out there.

She headed for the front door. The bell jingled again. Noelle shoved her hands into the jacket pockets and glanced around the diner.

Noelle tried to picture Jenny in her mind. Jenny's mother had brought a photograph of the girl to the station, and Jenny had certainly looked a lot like the images of the other girls they'd found.

A lot like me.

Jenny would've been working on that little sidewalk area. Excited and nervous because it was her first day. If someone had approached her, she would've just thought it was a customer, coming in early.

So you would've talked with him. Let him get close.

Close enough for him to attack her.

One set of footprints...

Her gaze slid to the right, toward the parking lot. The perp would've needed to be strong enough to carry Jenny away. And skilled enough to make sure Jenny never had the chance to cry out for help.

Noelle headed toward that parking lot. It was empty now, and the trees that surrounded the area swooped forward, arching in close.

It was a bitterly cold night, and the wilderness stretched as far as Noelle's eyes could see. If Jenny was out there, she could freeze to death during the night.

Provided the man who took her didn't *kill* her first.

Before she'd left the station, Noelle had heard the weather report come in—a bad winter storm was expected. Heavy snowfall. No one should be out on a night like this one, not with the storm coming. It was supposed to hit strongly just after midnight.

I don't want to find Jenny's frozen body tomorrow. I don't want to be the one who has to look into her mother's tear-filled eyes and tell her that her daughter isn't coming home again.

A twig snapped, the sound coming from the darkness about twenty feet in front of Noelle. She tensed as adrenaline flooded through her body. That sound could've been caused by an animal. It could've been caused by *anything*.

Even a perp who'd come back to the scene of his crime.

Noelle raced forward. Animal or man, she was about to find out exactly who she was dealing with out there. Her hands flew up, and she shoved aside the bushes in her path. She yanked out the flashlight she'd pushed into her coat earlier, and she whipped it up, shining the light.

No one was there.

At least, no one she saw.

But Noelle heard the rush of thudding footsteps, fleeing to the right.

She lunged that direction, but her feet got caught in something, and she twisted, falling down hard. Her left hand shoved into the snow and touched rough, frozen fabric. She yanked it up.

A scarf?

"Noelle!" Thomas's shout seemed to shake the trees.

She could still hear footfalls. She shined her light down. The snow was falling once more, but...

I see them.

She could see the outline left by a pair of boots. It wasn't an animal who'd been watching her in the darkness.

Was the scarf Jenny's? Maybe the perp hadn't taken Jenny away in a car. Maybe he'd just carried her off. Maybe Jenny was closer than they realized.

"Thomas, follow me!" Noelle called, and she didn't pause any longer. She raced right after that trail of footprints. The snow would just keep falling as the storm swept in and, soon, would obliterate the tracks. She couldn't let that watcher get away—not until she found out who the individual was and why that person was in the woods.

The innocent don't run.

But this guy was sure fleeing fast.

So she just had to be faster.

Chapter Five

Noelle had vanished into the woods. Thomas swore as he gave chase, shining his flashlight on the ground so he could follow her footprints.

He didn't know why she was running off, but he sure wasn't about to let her head out alone. Whatever she'd seen, Noelle was desperate to follow that lead.

And he was desperate to follow *her*.

His feet pounded into the snow. His boots were sinking into the soft fall, and the suction made every step that much harder.

He threw a fast glance over his shoulder. He couldn't see the lights from the diner, not anymore. There was darkness all around him and—

He glanced forward and his light hit Noelle. She stood in the middle of a clearing, with one of her hands locked around a flashlight and the other hand around her gun. Since she'd lost her own weapon in the icy water, she'd gotten that gun from the sheriff.

"There are two sets of tracks here," she said, voice tense.

His light flashed to the ground. "Who are we following? Did you get an ID on—"

"I didn't see him. I *heard* him, and I followed his footprints, but there are *two* sets now."

Two sets, which appeared to be the same size and shape.

"We have to split up," Noelle said, her words tumbling out. "I think the perp took Jenny into the woods. He didn't drive away with her. He carried her off. He's out here now, watching us."

Leaving a trail for them to follow?

Thomas's light fell over those prints again. The snowfall was getting harder.

"They'll be covered soon." She surged to the right. "You go left. I'll—"

He grabbed her arm, stopping her. "This is a trap." He knew it with certainty because he'd laid similar traps before.

Two sets of footprints to throw off those who pursued. To divide them up.

To make the attack easier.

"No, no, he's here. I heard him." She twisted her hand, trying to break loose from his hold and the light from her flashlight bobbed. But he didn't let her go. He *couldn't*. "Jenny won't survive if she's out in the open! We have to follow him, now!" She tugged again. "You go left. I'll go right."

He didn't let her go *anywhere*. "There's more snow to the left." The tracks were covered just a bit more. Because those tracks had been placed earlier? "We both go right."

And he led the way, with his flashlight positioned just over his gun. When it came to hunting deadly prey, Thomas was the one with more experience.

But I've been with her in the wilderness before. Noelle didn't remember that terrible night, but he did. There hadn't been any snow on the ground then. Just a hot, long southern night. A night of fear and death.

It was easy enough for a good hunter to cover his tracks, even out in the snow. Grab a branch, drag it behind you, and your trail was gone.

Whoever they were after... That person *wanted* them to follow.

Their prey was leading them somewhere. To Jenny? To death?

Thomas was about to show the fool he'd made a serious mistake.

Thomas was never the hunted. He'd been born to be the predator.

NOELLE EVERS WASN'T DEAD. She wasn't trapped beneath the frozen waters of the lake. She'd survived.

And she's hunting me.

He wanted to laugh, but sound carried too easily in the wilderness. He'd snapped that twig for her before because he'd just had to be sure, had to determine with one hundred percent certainty he was looking at Noelle.

The snow had fallen around her. Her red hair had been hidden under her cap. But when she'd called out—

I know her voice.

Noelle had changed so much over the years. Not easy prey any longer. Not like Jenny.

Noelle was following his trail. Hunting *him*.

She had a weapon. She had training. She was...

Perfect.

But Noelle wasn't alone. The other agent was with her. Moving like a shadow in the darkness. The man was a killer; he easily recognized the type. Instead of alarming him, the knowledge had his grin stretching even more.

And Lawrence had just wanted me to end them so quickly. Lawrence had never understood. It wasn't just about the kills. It was about the hunt.

He was about to enjoy the best hunt of his life.

Come to me, Noelle. Come in close, and let's see if I can make you scream the way I did before.

THE TRACKS ENDED—vanished into the rough edge of stone that lined the rising wall of a mountain.

"Where did he go?" Noelle spun around, shining her light. Her voice was high, nervous.

Thomas glanced up at the mountain. He suspected the man they were after had climbed up, which meant...

You know this area, well, don't you? How long have you been hiding in the Alaskan wilderness?

His light hit the edge of the mountain.

"Up there." Noelle's voice was fainter now as the wind began to howl more around them. The approaching storm was moving in fast. "We have to follow him!"

She tried to put her hands in the faint ridges between the icy rocks. Thomas pulled her back before she could climb. "We need to head back to town, Noelle."

Shaking her head, Noelle jerked away from him. "Jenny could be up there! We have to find her!"

"You can't scale the rocks." She thought she was going to free hand her way up that frozen

surface? Hell, no. She'd fall and break her neck.
"We'll go back to town and get help." Maybe
a chopper could fly them up the mountain.
They'd do a search. Look for any cabins that
would be a good base site for the man they
were after.

"We don't have time for that. Jenny needs
us!"

There was no sign of the man on the face of
the mountain. "He might not even be up there."
His gaze turned to the wilderness. "He could
be watching us, from out there."

Noelle shuddered. From cold? From fear?

"We're not equipped for this search. We need
supplies. Dogs."

"And Jenny needs us!" Noelle shook her
head. "I'm not just going to leave her."

"Are you going to die with her?" His words
were brutal, but Thomas had to make her see
reason.

Noelle gasped and lurched back a step.

"Because if we stay out in the open, if we
keep blindly following this man's path tonight
and that storm hits, you could die. You're already shaking apart in front of me, and hypo-
thermia will set in before you know it."

"She needs us," Noelle said again as her chin
notched up.

"And she could be anywhere. We're going

back for the dogs." He yanked out his phone, but of course, there was no cell service out here. Nothing.

Noelle's light hit to the left. To the right.

"I can't just leave her," Noelle told him.

She was going to *have* to leave her.

"You stay, you die with her." There was no way Thomas was going to let that happen on his watch. Even if he had to carry her out of there, Noelle was leaving the woods.

"I DON'T NEED you anymore." He let the knife trail over Jenny's skin. She was crying. Shaking. So useless to him. "You weren't what I was hoping for."

It had been because of Noelle. He'd gone a little…mad there for a moment. Forgotten all of his training. That wonderful training and control Lawrence had worked hard to give him over the years.

Lawrence had wanted to use him. He had. For so long.

But Lawrence had made a mistake.

They're my kills. My choice.

The knife cut through the gag that covered her mouth.

"P-please…" Jenny begged him. "Let…me go."

"It doesn't work like that."

"I won't tell anyone about you! *Please!*"

Ah, there she went. Making promises. But Jenny knew what he looked like. If she got to Noelle and the other agent, they'd want her to describe her abductor. They'd even sit her down with a sketch artist. Get her to come up with a composite of him.

Then his picture would be everywhere. The EOD would make sure of that.

I know all about the EOD, but they don't know about me. They have no clue just who— what—I am.

Their mistake. They thought the Jack of Hearts was the greatest threat they had to face. They were wrong. It was time to show them the error of their ways. Time for him to get all of the respect he had coming.

They'd thought Jack was a serial killer?

Jack was nothing.

He stroked the back of his hand over her cheek. "I have plans for you."

Jenny whimpered.

"I'M NOT LEAVING HER." Noelle shook her head, sending snowflakes falling around her. "You go back to town. You find the sheriff and get the dogs out here—"

Thomas shoved his gun into his holster and

let his flashlight's attached cord loop around his wrist as he grabbed both of her shoulders. "You think I'll just leave you out here to die alone? *We're partners!*"

She knew that. "She could be me," Noelle whispered as she stared up at his face. Her own light was hitting the ground, so she couldn't see his expression. "I was alone. I was trapped. The only person with me was a dead man."

His hold tightened on her.

"I was bound to a chair. If the cops hadn't found me…" A tip. They'd gotten a tip, which no one had ever been able to trace. "I could've died in that cabin." Starved to death, slowly. But Jenny wouldn't have to worry about death by starvation. Not when it was so bitterly cold outside.

She'll freeze to death by morning.

"You're not her." His voice was grim. "And I'll be damned if I let you die for her. You are coming with me. One way or—"

A scream ripped through the silence of the night.

Thomas stilled. Then, in the next instant, he'd torn away from Noelle. His gun was in his hand again as he rushed toward that dying sound.

A sound that hadn't come from high up on

the mountain, but one that had come from the right. Farther into the woods.

They fought their way through those trees, ran ahead even as another scream echoed in the night.

Then Noelle saw it. The hard, stark outline of a little cabin.

The cabin waited. The doors shut. "Please... please don't make me go back in there...."

Those words whispered through her mind. Noelle's *own* words, her broken voice, and she shook her head, hard, as she drew closer.

The cabin was pitch black. Thomas's flashlight hit the shut front door.

He ran toward it and kicked it in.

Another scream came then.

Noelle rushed in behind Thomas, providing cover for him. But there was no attacker in the room.

A young girl sat in the middle of the room, a rickety, wooden chair beneath her. Her arms were pulled behind her back. A blindfold covered her eyes.

The cabin was so familiar, for an instant, Noelle remembered... *"Please, I don't want to be alone! Don't leave me alone!"*

And a man's voice had replied to her.

He'd said, *"I'll always be with you."*

Hard shudders shook Noelle's body as the past and present seemed to merge around her.

Thomas crouched in front of the girl. "Jenny Tucker?"

She jerked. "Yes! Yes, help me!"

Noelle surged forward. She ran behind the girl and yanked until the binds around Jenny's wrists were gone. The girl's skin was icy. Her fingers... Her fingers were blue.

"H-he's c-coming back."

Thomas pulled the blindfold from Jenny's eyes. Jenny blinked up at him.

Noelle tugged Jenny to her feet. "He's not going to hurt you anymore. We're going to get you out of here."

Jenny shook her head. Tears slid down her cheeks. "I'm sorry..."

Noelle's nose burned. What was that acrid scent?

Her flashlight hit the walls. They looked... wet.

"We need to get out of here," Noelle yelled as she realized that, yes, Thomas had been right. They'd walked straight into a trap.

That smell—it was the heavy scent of gasoline.

Thomas picked Jenny up in his arms and sprinted for the door.

"H-he told me to scream…to scream until help came."

They were almost at the door but—

A blast seemed to shake the cabin. Fire blazed inside, rushing toward them, following the trail of fuel spread throughout the cabin.

Jenny screamed.

And the fire raged.

There was only one window in that cabin. One to the left, and fire already covered it. The front door was gone. A wall of flames stood in its place.

Thomas sat Jenny down on her feet. The girl immediately fell, and Noelle ran toward her, pulling her up before the flames could lick across the girl's skin.

Thomas shrugged out of his coat and wrapped it around Jenny's body. His gaze lifted and met Noelle's. "You get out first."

Uh, how?

"Cover up with your coat. Make sure none of your flesh is vulnerable." He coughed a bit because the smoke was rising fast. "The coat is going to ignite, so you'll have to strip and roll in the snow as soon as you get outside."

He wanted her to run *through* the fire. Right. But… "You don't have a coat." He'd just given his only protection to Jenny.

His jaw locked. The blaze let her see him clearly. "I'll be right behind you."

He'll burn. "Thomas…"

The flames flared higher. "Go!"

Tears stung Noelle's eyes.

"He could be waiting out there," Thomas warned her. "Get your gun, and cover me when I come out. I *need* you to get out there and cover me."

She was supposed to let him get hurt?

"Go, *Noelle, go…* I'll be right behind you."

And, over the roar of the fire, the voice from the darkness of her past spoke again. *I'll always be with you.*

A long tremor shook her body. Noelle ran toward the flaming doorway, and she jumped through the fire. There was a loud *whoosh* of sound, which seemed to fill her ears. Heat surrounded her, so hot, so—

Her body flew through the air, and she hit the snow. She rolled because Thomas had been right. Her clothes were on fire. She pushed out of her coat and kept rolling, then hurried back up to her feet, even as she pulled out her weapon.

I'm not burned. I'm not—

Thomas flew through the fire. The flames came with him when he left the cabin. He hit the snow, too, hard, and Jenny tumbled out of his hands. The coat Jenny wore was blazing. Noelle shoved it away, even as Jenny yelled for help.

Jenny wasn't burned, though; she was safe.

"Thomas?" Noelle whispered.

He yanked off the smoking ski mask he'd used to cover his face. He was twisting, trying to put out the fire consuming his clothes and pants.

Noelle helped him, securing her weapon and slapping at the blaze. Her gloves burned away.

The fire died.

Thomas glanced up at her.

"Are you hurt?" Noelle whispered. She didn't see any burns, but maybe it was just too dark to notice them.

He caught her hands. Her gloves were gone, only bits of fabric remained. "Are you?" Thomas demanded his voice an angry growl.

Noelle shook her head.

Somehow, they'd both made it out of that hell.

Jenny was sobbing.

Thomas rose to his feet. He picked Jenny up in his arms. "Watch my back," he told Noelle.

She had her weapon ready again. The killer had to be close. He'd set the fire just moments before, but...

It wasn't the time to chase after him. They

had to get Jenny to safety. Jenny was the key. She could help them identify her attacker.

Noelle hurried her steps and followed closely behind Thomas. His hold was gentle on Jenny. He had to be freezing, but he didn't slow at all. He was fast and strong, and his grip on the young woman was unbreakable.

For an instant, the snow-covered landscape vanished, and Noelle saw—

Not flames. Not snow. A forest. Woods. Noelle remembered the moonlight that had trickled through the tops of the trees. She'd stared up at it as he'd held her. His grip had been so strong. So solid. She'd been…safe.

Noelle's grip tightened on her gun as the image faded. She glanced back over her shoulder. The cabin was burning; the hungry flames consumed the place, destroying any evidence that might have been left behind.

But…

Jenny is safe. She survived.

Noelle was used to finding the bodies of the victims in her job as a profiler. She usually arrived too late to help anyone. But this… This was different.

We saved her.

She kept her gun up as she hastened after Thomas and Jenny.

I'll always be with you.

The voice whispered through her mind, and the voice—it belonged to Thomas.

JENNY WAS LOADED into the back of an ambulance. Thomas watched its lights flash on as the siren's cry filled the night. Jenny had been sobbing when she was loaded up. She'd told him again and again how sorry she was. *He made her lure us into that cabin—he wanted us all to burn.*

"I can't thank you two enough." Sheriff Hodges came toward him. He stared at Thomas, then Noelle with wide eyes. "That girl... You saved her."

They'd nearly died with her. Thomas looked back at the wilderness. "When are the dogs getting here?" Because every moment that passed was another moment the perp could use to flee.

"We can't send them out, not with the storm."

He'd been afraid of that. The snow was already falling so much harder, and the howl of the wind was constant now.

The sheriff ran a gloved hand over his face. "Word came through on the radio a little while ago. The storm's due to hit any minute. It won't be safe to send anyone out. The snow's gonna be too thick. The snowstorm will last all night."

And it would give the killer out there the perfect cover for his escape.

"Jenny wouldn't have lasted until dawn." Noelle's voice was soft. "If he hadn't killed her, then the storm would've."

Thomas could feel the push of the impending gales. As he'd carried Jenny, he'd fought to stay upright as the wind and the snow blasted against him.

"You two need to get secure for the night." Hodges gave a firm nod. "I'll get my men to check the area once more, but then I have to send them in. I won't lose any of my people for that guy."

No, they couldn't put lives on the line.

And so the perp gets away, for now.

The sheriff nodded once more, then turned away. The wind battered against Thomas. He was wearing a borrowed coat a sheriff's deputy had given him. Noelle was wearing a similar one, only its bulk seemed to swallow her.

She stared up at Thomas with unreadable eyes. Strange, he'd believed he'd gotten pretty good at reading Noelle's feelings. But right then, he couldn't tell a single thing about her thoughts.

Thomas cleared his throat. "We should get back to our place." Driving would be a nightmare if they waited much longer. It was a good thing their rented cabin was near town.

Noelle nodded, but she didn't move. "Do you jump through fire often?"

He hadn't expected the question. He felt his lips curl in a grim smile. "Only when I have to."

She inclined her head and spun, heading back toward the diner and their vehicle. Thomas saw Henry was out, watching them with wide eyes. The sheriff had taken the shovel in as evidence. Maybe they'd get lucky on the fingerprint check.

Maybe not.

But at least they'd found the girl.

When he'd rushed into that cabin and seen her there, the blindfold covering half her face, her red hair streaming behind him, it had been as if Thomas had run straight into a nightmare from his past.

Only I wasn't the white knight then.

He'd been the man ignoring the cries for help.

They reached their SUV. Snow coated the windows, and Thomas shoved it away. When the vehicle was clear—well, *clearer*—he glanced at Noelle. Her eyes were on him.

What is she thinking?

"I was wrong about you," Noelle said, and the howl of the wind nearly swallowed her words. "The profile that I had in my head… It was all wrong."

He stiffened at her words. "I warned you

before that you shouldn't profile me." Because he'd been afraid she wouldn't like the man who truly lived inside him.

"I just didn't realize how good you were at keeping secrets and telling lies."

She knows. "Noelle?"

She climbed into the vehicle. Thomas jumped inside with her. It was as cold in the SUV as it was outside. And the snow was falling in ever harder waves. He turned on the ignition. It took three tries for the motor to finally kick to life. The windshield wipers slashed across the glass, but they didn't help him see any better.

The sheriff had been right. Thomas figured he and Noelle would be lucky to make it back to their cabin before the storm hit with its full fury.

He spared another fast glance for Noelle. She was staring straight ahead, her attention seemingly on the snow that blasted down on them, but he could feel the tension emanating from her body.

Oh, yeah, the storm was about to hit, and he had a feeling it just might wreck his world.

HE'D LEARNED TO cover his tracks when he was ten years old. But he didn't slow down to erase his footprints. There was no need then. Mother Nature was erasing the tracks for him.

The fire was out. He didn't even see the smoke drifting up into the sky any longer.

He'd watched the blaze, just for a moment, and he'd seen them escape.

Worthy prey.

Noelle had come out first. She'd been burning. He'd smiled at the sight. But the flames had been extinguished all too quickly. The male had followed her—and he'd brought out Jenny.

Jenny shouldn't have made it out of the house.

Now two have survived.

That wasn't acceptable. He'd have to correct that situation.

Jenny would be easy enough. She didn't have any fight in her. But Noelle... Now, there was his challenge. He'd take her out first. Her and the agent who seemed to always be at her side. The fellow thought he was some sort of protector. No, he was just a dead man walking, and he didn't know it.

He'd kill Noelle and her shadow.

It was just that the *shadow* had seemed familiar to him. Something about the man's profile. His voice. *I feel like I know him.*

His breath heaved from his lungs. The snow fell harder.

A storm...it would be the perfect cover.

When the snow fell so heavily, no one would be looking for an attack.

No one would see him. Not until it was too late.

Chapter Six

The snow pelted down on their cabin. Noelle pulled the oversize coat closer to her body as she glanced back over her shoulder. Thomas shoved the door closed, pushing his shoulder into the wood, then securing the lock.

It was cold inside, but cold wasn't the reason why Noelle was shivering.

Her past was coming back to her, and the images that kept flashing through her mind didn't make any sense. They couldn't be real. Not unless—

"I'll get the fire going," Thomas said as he stalked toward the large fireplace. "You should head upstairs. Get in a warm shower. Wash away the ash and get some feeling back in your limbs."

There was no emotion in his words, and he wasn't looking directly at her. She found, right then, she couldn't take her gaze off him.

He bent near the fireplace. A few moments later, flames flashed up.

A shudder shook her as she remembered the fire that had nearly taken their lives.

Still crouching, Thomas glanced back at her. The gold of his gaze reminded her of the fire. "Go on upstairs," he said again. "You're shaking."

"It's not from the cold." Well, okay, perhaps part of it was. She crept closer to him and to the warmth of the fireplace. Her hands were fisted in the pockets of her borrowed coat. "I need to ask you some questions."

He looked toward the stairs. "The power might not stay on long, not if the storm is as strong as I'm thinking it will be. You should shower first, then we can talk."

She braced her legs and straightened her shoulders. She'd waited long enough for this conversation. "Tell me about the first time that we met."

His eyelids flickered as he slowly rose to his full height. He wasn't looking at the stairs any longer. He was focused on her, and his stare was guarded. "Why does that matter?"

"Because I… I remember your voice."

His jaw hardened.

"I can hear your voice in my head. You're saying that…you'll always be with me."

He didn't speak.

"But you've never said those words to me."

He turned back toward the fire.

"At least, you haven't said them since I started with the EOD. So that means you had to tell them to me *before* Mercer brought me on." She was trying to keep her voice even and calm, but her heart was galloping like mad in her chest. "And the only *before* for me, the only time I don't remember, is the forty-eight hours of my abduction."

He looked back at her. His expression was unreadable. "You've had one hell of a night. We both have. After you've slept, I bet things will be clearer for you."

"Doctors told me that same line for weeks." Anger snapped in her words, and she tried to pull back the old fury. "'Things will be clear…' and 'Give it some time…' and 'You just need rest.'" Her laughter held a bitter edge. "I've heard all of that a dozen times before. And guess what? Rest doesn't help. Time doesn't help." Her lips pressed together, and after a tense moment, Noelle demanded, "But you know what *did* help? Seeing that poor girl tied to the chair." She took a step toward him. *"Just like me."* Because it had been as if she'd stared into a mirror of her past.

A muscle flexed along Thomas's jaw. "She's

not you, though, Noelle. You're just getting things confused."

She sucked in a sharp breath. "Stop lying to me."

He shook his head.

"You are. You're lying. From the moment I saw you at the EOD, I felt like we'd met before."

"Other missions," he growled out. "Our paths have crossed. I can't tell you what I was doing then; you don't have the clearance."

"Forget clearance!" The words came out as a yell as she shot forward and grabbed his arms. "This is my life! Tell me!"

He stared into her eyes. "I've seen you. You haven't always seen me. The FBI works plenty of cases that merge with the EOD. Sometimes, you guys thought you were hunting serials, but you were after assassins. It was our job to contain those killers. My team did its job."

"No, there's more to this." Earlier, she was sure that he'd started to tell her more. Back at the station, before they'd learned about Jenny.

"I've told you the truth."

Her temples were throbbing, her heart breaking. "Not all of it." She blinked because her eyes were filling with tears, and she would *not* let them fall. "I thought we were partners. I thought we could count on each other." She dropped her hold and stepped back. "I guess I thought wrong." She whirled away from him.

But his hand locked around her shoulder, and he spun her right back to face him.

"Thomas—"

His mouth crashed down on hers. She was so shocked by the move she just stood there a moment. Then…

"Damn it, I'm sorry." He tore his mouth from hers, but he didn't let her go. Thomas stared down at her with glittering eyes. "Let's try that again…."

And this time, the kiss was softer. Tempting her, not taking or demanding, but seducing her instead.

Her emotions were about to rip her apart. She shouldn't just be standing in his arms.

I'll always be with you. The memory of those words didn't scare her. The words made her feel safe. The way being with Thomas always did.

Her hands rose to curl around his shoulders. She shouldn't be in his arms, no, but nothing had ever felt more right to her before.

His mouth pressed to hers, and her lips parted. He kissed her, deeply, sensually, and she rose onto her toes in front of him. The anger that had been blasting through her changed. Desire rose, igniting like a firestorm because, suddenly, it was all too much. The past. The present. The fire. The fear.

She didn't want to think anymore. She only wanted to feel. And Thomas, he was very, very good at making her feel.

Her hands shoved against his coat. He let her go, just for a moment, and that coat hit the floor. He stared at her, and she could read his gaze then, no problem. Lust and heavy desire shined in his eyes. "Noelle…"

She shook her head. She'd asked him to talk. He'd refused. Now… Now she just wanted to keep feeling.

Noelle tossed aside her coat. Kicked off her boots and ditched her socks. She was stripping in front of him, when she'd never had the courage to do this before, not in front of the only two lovers she'd had. She'd been so nervous with them. So afraid.

But there wasn't any room for fear. Not with him.

Thomas pulled her against him and kissed her again, even as his hands slid over her flesh. His fingertips were rough, callused, but he was so careful as he caressed her. She arched into his touch. Wanting more. Needing more. She needed everything he had to give.

Lies. Truth. She didn't know the line between them anymore.

She didn't know what was memory. What was hope. She only knew desire.

He pulled her down onto the rug in front of the fireplace. She could hear the wind howling outside. She could feel the mad drumbeat of her heart, shaking her from the inside.

He ditched his clothes, and then he—he just gazed down at her.

"You're the most perfect thing that I've ever seen."

No, she wasn't. Her breasts were too small. Her legs too long and—

He bent his head and took her nipple into his mouth. A surge of heat had her gasping his name. He kept kissing her breast, licking her nipple, even as his hand slid down her body. Her legs spread for him, and his fingers explored her flesh.

"Warm," his voice rumbled against her, "so…*hot and perfect.*"

She felt as if she were burning then. The cold was long gone. Her breath heaved out in pants as he took his time learning her body. Stroking. Licking. Touching.

Kissing.

Everywhere.

Her nails bit into his shoulders. It had never been like this for her before. The passion so intense, her body responding so quickly. Maybe it was the adrenaline. The fear. The fury.

Or maybe it was just the man.

He positioned himself between her legs. His eyes blazed and—

"I need to protect you..."

Understanding dawned for her. She shook her head. "I'm safe." She was on contraception, and she was clean. All of the agents underwent regular physicals and—

"I'm clean," he gritted out, "and I want you... more than I've ever wanted anyone or anything."

"Then take me," she heard herself whisper.

His fingers caught hers and he pinned her hands to the rug. He stared into her eyes, his face a mask of stark need as he thrust inside her.

He drove deep and filled her completely. She gasped at the sensation because it had been so long for her, and sex with her other lovers had never been like this.

Heat. Need. Passion.

He withdrew. Plunged deep. Again and again. Her legs wrapped around his hips as she surged up to meet his thrusts. Every hard glide of his body pushed him right over her sensitive core, and her body tightened. Release was close, so very close and—

Noelle screamed when the pleasure hit her. No gentle wave. No crest of release. But an avalanche, which rolled right over her, stealing her breath and making her heart slam into her ribs. She cried out Thomas's name, so lost in him she could barely see. Her body trembled, spasmed and she held on to him as fiercely as she could.

Then he drove into her once more. He stiffened, and the growl that broke from him was her name.

She tried to focus on him because she wanted to see him in that moment. The hard angles of his face. The pleasure in his eyes.

He bent toward her. He kissed her.

And he kept thrusting.

Her breath caught and she arched toward him. Because she realized the pleasure wasn't over.

It was just beginning.

WHEN NOELLE OPENED her eyes, she was still by the fire. The rest of the house was dark, but the fire blazed. Thomas was in front of the hearth, wearing a pair of jeans. He bent forward as she watched and he stirred up the flames.

"The power's out," he said, without looking back at her.

A soft cover surrounded her body. She didn't

even know where that cover had come from, but she pulled it closer.

"We should stay down here," Thomas said, his attention seemingly on the blaze. "It's warmer here, as long as we keep the fire going."

Keeping the blanket with her, Noelle sat up. She brought her knees in front of her and watched Thomas.

"I didn't…mean for that to happen." His voice was low, rasping, and his shoulders were tense. "I know I pounced on you and—"

"If this is the part where you apologize," she said, a bit surprised by the bite in her own voice, "don't. I knew exactly what I was doing and exactly what I wanted."

He looked back at her.

"You," Noelle told him simply. "I wanted to be with you."

He swallowed. She saw the faint movement of his Adam's apple. "There are things you don't know about me."

She lifted her brows at that. "I'd say I know you pretty well by now." Biblically well.

He glanced toward the fire once more. "You know what you read in the files Mercer gave you, but with me… He wouldn't have shown you everything."

Noelle forced herself to take slow, deep breaths. "And why not?"

The flames crackled.

"My father was a solider." Thomas spoke slowly. "He was a damn good fighter and a good man." His hand lifted and he stared at it for a second. Then he struck out with a powerful force that seemed to whip through the air around him. His hand was perfectly straight as it moved in a series of fast, hard glides—attacks that were both beautiful…and brutal. "He taught me how to fight when most kids were learning how to read and write. He wanted me to be prepared, always prepared for what life might throw at me."

She waited.

"My mother didn't like being a soldier's wife. She left, and she took me with her." His jaw hardened. "And he died on his next mission."

"I'm sorry." The words felt so hollow to her.

"My dad was good at what he did. His walls were full of medals and commendations. But when he lost us, I think he just stopped caring." He rubbed a hand over his face. "I realized then just how dangerous love could be to a man. Love makes you weak. Vulnerable."

She shook her head, even though he couldn't see the move. "It doesn't have to be like that."

"It does…when love becomes an obsession. When it's all you think about. When you can't do your mission because you're seeing a woman in your head. You're worried about her, thinking about her, and you can't protect your team, much less yourself."

She didn't know what to say then.

"I intended to live my life without any commitments. The missions *were* my life, and women... Sex was a necessity I took care of when I needed it."

Noelle stiffened. Her hold on the cover tightened. Okay, he'd better not have just said she was some kind of itch he'd *taken care of.* The man needed to think again. He wasn't—

He faced her. "You're different, and I can't afford the weakness that you make me feel."

That was both good *and* insulting. "I'm not a weakness to you."

"Yes," he said softly. "You are. More than you know." He rolled back his shoulders. "I should've known once wouldn't be enough with you."

She distinctly remembered at least two times. During the third, she'd—

"I should have kept my hands off you, but I couldn't."

Noelle cleared her throat. "I didn't want them off. I wanted you."

He shook his head. "No, you just wanted to stop being afraid, and I was close and convenient."

Oh, the hell *no,* he hadn't just said that.

Noelle jumped to her feet. The cover almost fell, so she scrambled to keep it over her. Then she stalked toward Thomas, and she jabbed him in the chest with her index finger. "Listen up, soldier," Noelle snapped at him.

His brows lifted.

"You are many things, but trust me, convenient isn't one of them." Not by a long shot. "You're infuriating, you're secretive and you're deadly. *Convenient* doesn't even make your top-ten list."

"Then why were you with me? Why did you give yourself to me?" The words held a hard demand.

She licked her lips and swore she could still taste him. "Because I needed you right then…" She thought of his words. "More than I needed anyone or anything." Even the secrets of her past. Secrets her gut told her he knew.

He didn't speak. Maybe he was back to being Strong and Silent. That was okay. Noelle found she had plenty to say. "What happened between us tonight wasn't about the past. It was only about the present. About me needing you. About you needing me. I'm not looking for forever." Was that why he was giving her the spiel about sex being a necessity? She straightened her shoulders and vowed not to crumble. "I just needed you, because when you look at me—"

and she'd seen this in his gaze "—you see *me*. Flaws. Strengths. You seem to see all of me, and you want what you see."

He didn't realize how important that was to her. She felt broken on the inside, but he looked at her with such hunger, such desire.

Maybe it was time for them to be completely honest. They were alone in the cabin. Separated from the rest of the world by the storm. "I know you were there," she whispered.

Because Noelle was watching him so closely, she saw the slight hardening of his mouth.

"It's not me being confused. I hear your voice, and I know you were there when I was taken." There had been so many law enforcement personnel swarming the little cabin when she was rescued. Had he been a deputy back then? A face that she couldn't remember, but a voice that had stayed with her? "What I don't understand is…why…after everything, you just won't admit the truth to me. It's my life. I should have the highest possible clearance when it comes to *me*."

His hand rose. The back of his fingers brushed over her cheek. He swallowed and whispered, "I was there."

It took an instant for those words to sink in. "When the rescuers came for me?"

His eyes closed. "I saw you in my mind for

years after that night. I hated to leave you, but I didn't have a choice. The mission I was on meant that I couldn't be compromised. Other lives were at stake."

Her heart should have been racing. Instead, its beat was slow. Everything felt slow for her right then. "You didn't answer my question."

His eyes opened.

"Were you there when the rescuers came?" She remembered a deputy, a guy with a wide-brimmed hat who'd pulled her from the chair and guided her from the cabin. After she'd gotten outside, the deputy had vanished. But he'd been...good to her. He'd pulled her from the darkness and—

Thomas shook his head.

Her heart stopped then. "Thomas?"

"I was told never to talk about that night."

She couldn't have this conversation covered only in a blanket. And she couldn't leave the room right then, not if her life depended on it. "Who told you?"

"Mercer."

The puppet master. The man always pulling the strings. The man who'd been in and out of Noelle's life for years. *"Why?"*

"Because EOD agents can't be compromised, you know that."

She had to figure this out before she shattered. "You're thirty-seven."

His head inclined toward her.

"Fifteen years ago…you would have only been twenty-two." The background file Mercer had given to her had indicated Thomas hadn't joined the EOD until he was twenty-seven, after he'd spent years working operations as an Army Ranger.

"I was twenty-two, and I'd been killing for the government for years by then."

"You weren't EOD." He *couldn't* have been.

Thomas simply stared back at her.

"Tell me!"

"I've been with the EOD since I was twenty-one years old." His lips twisted. "I told you, I was very, very good at my job."

A wave of dizziness had her stepping back from him. "Mercer knows what happened to me, too, doesn't he?" He's known, and for years, he's said nothing.

Thomas nodded.

"Why? It's my life!" Anger was cracking through her.

"But other lives were on the line. We thought… We thought your abduction was an isolated incident." He tried to reach out for her, but she flinched back. "I didn't know there were other girls involved, not until we found those pictures."

Had Mercer known? Was that why he'd been so adamant she investigate the senator? "Tell me everything."

"Clearance—"

"Don't!" How dare he throw that up to her? "You just made love to me. There were no barriers between us. It was you and it was me." She heaved out a breath. Her heart wasn't beating slowly anymore. It was thundering in her chest. "I've had a void in my mind for years. A void that you could fill. All you had to do was speak. Just…tell me." She was about to rip that cover in two with her grip. "Do it now, Thomas. Tell me. I'm not crazy. I remember your voice, I remember—"

"You were in the woods." His voice was flat. Ice cold. "I heard your screams, so I ran to investigate."

Her knees almost gave way. She grabbed for the mantel and kept one hand around the cover that shielded her.

His hands were fists at his sides. "You were fleeing in the woods. You were hysterical, crying, saying that a man was chasing you." The faint lines around his mouth deepened in the firelight. *"Hunting you."*

Goose bumps rose on her skin.

"I didn't see anyone, and you… You were too pale. Your pupils were dilated, and I thought— I thought you were on drugs. At first."

She could only shake her head. But…the doctors *had* thought she'd been drugged. *Rohypnol.* Since it could cause memory loss, that had been the drug they suspected the most. *And* since it could be untraceable in the blood after the passage of time, they'd figured her abductor must have given it to her.

"Then I saw your hands. You had bruises around your wrists. As if you'd been tied up. Restrained."

Her lungs were starving for air, even though she was breathing as deeply as she could.

"I never expected to find you in those woods. Saving you… It wasn't my mission, but… *I wasn't going to let anyone hurt you.*"

"They found me in the cabin." His story wasn't making sense to her. She'd been in the cabin, not out in the open, in the woods.

"Because I took you back there."

She stumbled away from the mantel. "I was tied up! *You* did that to me?"

He tried to grab her, but even though she'd craved his touch before, she couldn't stand it right then.

And she needed clothes.

Clothes!

She spun away from him. Grabbed a flashlight and then she was running up the stairs.

"Noelle!"

Her world was shaking, and she wasn't going to stand there, naked. She shoved open the door to her bedroom. Her flashlight hit on the bed. It was so cold in there. Icy.

She grabbed for her suitcase, even as she heard him thundering up the stairs behind her. She yanked on her jeans. Pulled on a T-shirt. Didn't slow down for underwear. Her teeth were chattering. So cold. So cold because—

The window was open.

Noelle froze.

"We've started, and we aren't stopping," Thomas said as he stormed into her room. "Mercer is going to fire my ass, but I don't care. I won't hold back with you any longer. After what happened tonight, I can't."

Her flashlight was on the window. "Why is it open?" It shouldn't be open. It had been locked when they'd left before.

Her light hit the floor. Snow was inside, some melted, some still a hard white.

"Where's your weapon?" Thomas asked her, voice whisper soft.

The window was open, and it looked... It almost looked as if there were wet boot prints on the hardwood floor.

"Downstairs." There was no way someone could've gotten into the cabin, not while they were there and…making love.

Would I even have noticed an intruder then? No.

Thomas's hand closed around her arm. "You stay next to me, got it?" He didn't have his weapon, either. Both guns… They were downstairs. They'd put them aside in their frantic need for each other.

She turned toward Thomas. "Are we alone?" The storm was still raging. The wind was so strong. Maybe—maybe the window had just blown open. She pulled away from Thomas and went toward that window. Shut it. Locked it.

And Thomas was right by her, moving to keep his body beside hers. "We're about to find out," he told her, voice still low and soft. "You stay with me, and we're going to do a full-house sweep."

"*After* we get our weapons." His words about her past were swirling through her mind, but this…new fear was within her. Jenny's abductor had gotten away. Had he come after them? They went back down the stairs on silent feet. The shadows seemed to stretch all around them.

Noelle's skin crawled at the thought of someone being in that cabin with them, watching them while they made love.

Thomas's gun was just where he'd left it. So was hers. When the gun was in Noelle's hands, she finally felt better. They checked the cabin, moving room by room.

But no one was there.

No other windows were open.

It must've just been the storm. The wind…

Thomas headed toward the cabin's back door.

"What are you doing?" Noelle asked him.

He spared her a brief glance as he shouldered into his coat. He'd already donned his shirt and boots. "I'm checking the exterior perimeter."

Noelle shook her head. "In this storm? You need to stay inside." *And you need to finish telling me what really happened that long-ago night.*

But his jaw was locked and his body radiated determination. "The window was open. I'm making damn sure someone didn't open it. I want to check outside and see if there are any signs of an intruder."

"There won't be any signs. The snow would've covered any signs."

He motioned toward her gun. "Keep your weapon close until I get back."

No. He wasn't walking out into that storm without her. "If you're going, then so am I."

Thomas shook his head. "I need you to stay inside. The weather is going to be rough enough as it is. One of us has to make sure the interior of this place remains secure."

"But—"

But he wasn't listening to her.

Thomas was already gone.

Chapter Seven

Thomas mentally cursed himself as he trudged through the snow. He should never have lowered his guard. For someone to get close enough to the house...to get *inside* while he was there... Thomas knew he was seriously slipping. That didn't happen. He was always aware of his surroundings and of any threats that were close.

But when Noelle had kissed him back, when she'd responded so wildly, he'd lost control. He'd taken what he'd wanted for so long.

And he'd been blind to everything else.

Then...hell, he'd revealed too much. Mercer would nail his hide to the wall, but Thomas didn't care. Noelle deserved to know what was happening. *Especially* if the past was coming back—and it sure looked as if it was.

He headed around the cabin and shined his light up near Noelle's window.

Snow covered the area once more, and there

was no sign up there anyone had been climbing on the cabin. No sign but…

His light lowered. It hit the ground. The snow was blowing wildly around him, flying hard. He turned to the left because over the howl of the wind, he'd thought he'd heard—

His light fell on the shadowy form of man. A man who stood less than fifteen feet away from him. The man was bundled up, with a thick ski mask covering his face.

He stared at Thomas for an instant, then he spun away.

"Stop!" Thomas snarled.

But the man didn't stop. He ran into the thick snow, heading for the line of trees.

And Thomas hurried after him as he fought the grasping hold of the snow.

THE THUNDER OF a gunshot rose over the howling of the wind.

Noelle lunged for the door when she heard that sound. Forget securing the interior of the cabin. Thomas needed her!

She already had on her borrowed coat, and she rushed for the door with her flashlight in one hand and her gun in the other. She didn't have on gloves, and the wind whipped against her skin.

"Thomas!" The gale seemed to yank the cry away from her.

Another gunshot rang out. It sounded as though it had come from the line of trees near the east. She fought the snow and struggled in that direction.

Her light flew around. She didn't see Thomas and couldn't see anything but the line of trees and a haze of white as the snow spun in the air.

Thomas wasn't answering her call. Had he been the one firing? Or had someone been shooting at him?

She pushed into the shadows of the trees. The cold was already making her body shake. Her fingers had a death grip on the flashlight and the gun.

A shadow rushed to the side, moving in the corner of her light. She spun to the left. *"Thomas?"*

Then something hit her. No, *someone*. The tackle sent Noelle flying into the snow. She shoved up with her elbow, ready to break her assailant's nose.

"It's me!"

Thomas's voice.

"He's got a gun, baby, so be careful." He rose then. He didn't have a light, and hers had slipped from her grip. She floundered, trying to find it, but he caught her hand. "The light just makes us a bigger target."

Noelle thought she heard laughter then, tangled with the howl of the wind.

Thomas pulled away from her. He seemed to be swallowed by the thick snow. She scrambled to her feet. Her eyes were narrowed as she struggled to keep him in her line of sight, but he was moving quickly, even in that thick curtain. Heading deeper into the woods as he followed his prey.

Someone was in the house with us. Someone saw...

"I remember you..."

Did she hear those words? Imagine them? The storm was so loud.

"Noelle..." Something brushed over her arm, and she jumped as she spun around.

But... No one was there.

Her attention jerked back toward Thomas. He'd just rushed into a thick copse of trees. She hurried after him.

And tripped, slamming right into the ground.

Swearing, she fought to rise again, but her fingers caught the—the rope that had been hidden near her feet. Rope that had been used to trip her.

A trap. For prey.

For them.

"Thomas!" Noelle screamed. "Stop! It's a setup!" The window, the shots… They were designed to lure them out into this wilderness.

She pushed onto her knees, then staggered after Thomas. He hadn't heard her cry. He hadn't stopped. She had to get to him.

Noelle shoved through the line of trees, and a hand grabbed her arm. She saw the thick outline of a man before her, a man covered in winter clothing, but—

Not Thomas.

She fired her weapon. The bullet hit him, she knew it did. This close, there was no way she could miss, but he didn't let her go. He tightened his hold on her and yanked her forward.

And he—he *threw* her.

Noelle screamed once more, but the wind was wailing around her. She expected to hit the snow when she fell, but she hit something hard instead.

Ice.

And she felt that ice begin to splinter beneath her hand.

The sound of laughter seemed to float on the wind once more.

"Noelle!"

Thomas. That wasn't laughter; that was *his* frantic voice.

She looked up. He was fighting to get close

to her. *"Don't!"* She tried to yell as loudly as she could. She raised her arm toward him.

And felt more of the ice crack beneath her.

"Stay back!" Could he hear her? "It's giving way! We'll both—"

The ice broke, and Noelle fell into the frigid water. It was so cold it stole her breath. Her feet and legs seemed to go numb right away. She couldn't move them, couldn't kick. Her arms had flown out in front of her when the ice broke, and they were still above the surface. She slapped them down on the frozen plane, hoping to find a way to secure herself because she was going down. Her heart was racing. The water was freezing her.

"I've got you!" Fingers wrapped around hers.

Her gaze flew up. She could barely make out Thomas's form. He was lying on the ice, his body spread out. His fingers were around hers, but she couldn't feel his touch.

She couldn't feel anything but that Arctic water, and it was pulling her down.

"I'm getting you out!" He was yelling, but his words sounded like a whisper. "We have to keep our weight distributed. Don't stand up when you're clear...."

He was pulling her up. Inch by slow, desperate inch.

He thought she was planning to stand? Her

legs weren't working, her teeth were chattering, and she was afraid she'd pass out at any moment.

But he kept pulling her. Slowly. Carefully. Her hips hit something solid. She could feel new splinters in that surface beneath her. *"H-hurry..."* Noelle managed to rasp because she was terrified more of the ice was about to give way. If she and Thomas both went in, they wouldn't come out.

He didn't hurry. He kept up that inching pace. Her whole body shuddered with cold. Her hands were numb in his grasp. Her face was against the ice. The cracks scratched her skin.

"We're almost there, baby. Hold on for me."

She wasn't holding on to him at all. She couldn't.

"Got you!" Thomas yanked her forward and into his arms. He fiercely held her. She should feel the warmth from his body. She didn't. Tremors shook her. Her gaze fell on the shadows behind them as Thomas tried to rub her arms and her legs. He was yanking at her wet clothes.

"B-behind..." Speaking was so hard. She tried to push at him. To warn him.

Thomas was too fixated on her.

"G-gun..." Where was his weapon? They needed it.

Thomas's head flew up.

"B-behind…"

He pushed her down into the snow. His hand hit the ground near her and when it rose again, she saw he had his weapon. He fired. Once. Twice.

She'd seen the shadow out there watching them. Waiting for another moment to attack.

"He's running," Thomas snarled.

"F-follow…" The man had already gotten away once. They couldn't afford to let him vanish again.

"If I do, you're dead." He pulled her into his arms and kept his gun ready. "No, baby, that's not happening. You're priority."

She needed to help him. The attacker could circle back around. Everything that was happening… It was all one big trap. She had to help Thomas.

But she could only shudder.

He pulled her closer. "I've got you, and I won't let you go…"

THE SNOW WAS a blur around him. The agent had Noelle. He was trying to make his way back to the cabin with her.

His chest burned where Noelle's bullet had hit him. The blood was leaving a trail in the snow. But the storm would make that trail vanish. The storm would…

He leaned against a tree as he fought to catch his breath. The man's bullet had grazed his arm, cutting through the coat, but Noelle's had been the one to do the most damage. He'd just been caught off-guard by her. To see her, standing right in front of him, after all of those years…

She was a ghost from his past.

A ghost who had *shot* him. He'd reacted instinctively when the bullet hit. He'd grabbed her and thrown her toward the ice.

The ice had been meant for the man—the one called Thomas. The fellow was proving himself to be a worthy hunter.

But he'd still die.

And I remember you, Thomas… Because he'd crossed paths with that man before. Only Thomas hadn't been such a *good* guy then. Noelle had no clue about the man she thought was her partner.

No. Clue.

Thomas would die soon. So would Noelle.

It was just a matter of time….

The wound throbbed. He shoved more snow against it. Damn it, he was going to have to stop that bleeding. He could feel weakness pushing through his blood. But where the hell was he supposed to find help in this storm?

Gritting his teeth, he trudged forward. He'd stayed alive through plenty of attacks. He'd survive this, too, and then...then he'd make Noelle Evers and her partner *pay*.

"NOELLE? BABY, LOOK AT ME." Thomas yanked the wet clothing off Noelle and tossed the items away. He'd made it back to the cabin with her. He'd locked the doors, secured the place in seconds, and now he was trying to get her warm again.

Her lips were totally devoid of color. Her face far too pale. Her skin was icy beneath his touch, and shudders racked her.

"It's okay," he told her, aware his voice was ragged. "I've got you." Fear still raced through his veins. When she'd gone through the ice, he'd been terrified he wouldn't be able to get her out in time.

"T-Thomas?"

"Yes, baby, I've got you." He knew he was just repeating himself, but he didn't care. He settled her on the rug in front of the fireplace and wrapped the blanket around her. Her fingers fumbled as she tried to hold up the fabric.

Get her warm. Keep her safe. Those were his two priorities. He stoked the fire, building up the flames, then he stripped as quickly as he could. But Thomas made sure to keep his gun close by. He was pretty certain the perp they wanted was still out in that storm, but he wasn't going to take any chances.

He wanted to search the whole cabin again, but he couldn't, not until he took care of Noelle.

He turned back to her. The blanket had slipped down to her hips.

"Baby…" He dropped beside her and pulled her close. He stretched out with her, and he wrapped his body around hers as best he could. Flesh to flesh. His body could warm hers. He positioned the blanket around her and he just… He just held her. Held her and tried to fight the gnawing fear in his stomach.

He'd stared down terrorists, looked into the barrel of a loaded gun during a particularly brutal game of Russian roulette.

He'd battled through hellfire.

But he'd never been as afraid as he'd been when she screamed his name and fell through the ice.

Never again. He had to find that SOB out there. He had to stop him before the man came after Noelle once more.

His hands slid over her back. She was shivering, and her lips were pressed against his neck. He wanted to take all of her pain away.

He wanted to do anything, everything to protect her.

Yet the only thing he could do was hold her. Hold her and try to give her his warmth.

The fire crackled, and gradually, the shivers eased from her body. His hands curled around her hips. She felt warmer. At least, he hoped she did.

"Thank you…" Her soft whisper blew against his neck. "I was…a-afraid I wasn't getting out of the water."

His hold tightened on her. "I never would've left you." If necessary, he would've gone in that water and found a way to pull her out.

He'd left her once before. Followed orders, even though every instinct he possessed had screamed against it. He wouldn't make that mistake ever again.

Her lips pressed against his throat. The lightest of caresses.

Thomas swallowed. "You should…probably not do that."

When she'd been shivering with cold, they'd had to be close *and* naked for survival.

But she was warmer, and he—he *always* wanted her.

She kissed his neck again. *"Thank you."* He felt the light lick of her tongue against his skin.

His eyes squeezed shut. The woman didn't

seem to realize just how fragile his control was. When it came to her, hell, he couldn't *keep* control in place. Not a possibility.

Her legs shifted against him, parted so her thighs were on either side of his.

Bad, bad mistake. "Noelle…"

She kissed him again. He'd never realized how sensitive his neck was. When Noelle kissed him there, when she licked him with that delicate little tongue of hers, a wave of arousal shot right through his body. He was already hard for her, with her naked body rubbing against his, how could he not be? But now…

My control is shredding.

"I want in you," he told her, and he didn't see how he could be more blunt. "So you need to pull away. You're weak, you need to rest and—"

Her head lifted. The fire had dried her damp hair. He could see the shine of her eyes. "I want you in me," she said softly.

And he was lost.

His hands slid around her body, found the center of her need. He caressed her. Felt that last thread of his control give way—

Thomas thrust into her—drove into her until he was hilt deep. She might have been cold before, but right then, she was blazing hot. Her sex clamped tightly around him, and Thomas was pretty sure he was about to lose his mind.

Noelle pushed up, bracing her hands against the floor. Her breasts were so close, he had to lean up and take one into his mouth.

Then she started moving. Rising. Falling. The rhythm was maddening. He needed more. He needed deeper, but Noelle was going slow. Slow and sensual. Every glide of her body had his muscles aching with the effort to hold back.

He wanted to take, and he would, but first… *Noelle.*

He kept stroking the center of her need. He knew now just how she liked to be touched. Knew the caresses she needed. Knew just how to make her eyes go blind and to make her gasp.

When she moaned his name, he smiled.

When she came, crying out, her body tensing, he took over.

His hands locked tightly around her hips. He lifted her body, up and down, again and again, driving in the rhythm he needed. When it wasn't enough, when he needed more, deeper, he twisted with her, putting her beneath him on that rug.

And he took her. Claimed her. Pleasure flooded through him.

He kissed her when the release erupted.

Kissed her and tasted life and hope. Tasted everything he'd ever wanted.

Thomas knew that, in an instant, he would kill to keep her by his side.

THE STORM HAD PASSED. Noelle stared out at the sea of white around the cabin. In the distance, she could hear the rumble of snowplows.

The road in front of their cabin was covered, but she knew they'd be getting out of there soon enough.

Her gaze slid toward the trees that lined the property. Had the perp survived the night? She bet he had. But...

"My bullet hit him," she said quietly. Thomas was behind her. Not talking. They hadn't talked much during the remainder of the night.

They'd made love, and exhausted, she'd fallen asleep in his arms. When she'd woken up, he'd been dressed. Armed.

And the day had dawned.

"I grazed him," Thomas said, as he drew closer to her. "Or at least, I think I did."

Her shot had been at near point-blank range, so Noelle figured the wound she'd inflicted had to be bad. "He'll need medical help." She glanced toward Thomas. "I hit him in the chest. Not his heart, but enough of a wound that the guy can't just keep walking around without treatment." Not even close. "*If* he survived the storm, he'll be looking for someone to patch him up." So they'd check first with local doctors and veterinary personnel. Someone with medical training.

"He'll look, unless he's the kind of man used to taking care of his own wounds."

Noelle thought of the scars on Thomas's body. "You've done that."

"When it comes down to either being able to stitch up yourself or dying, yeah, you learn to stitch that skin pretty fast." His voice was grim. "I've dug bullets out. Hell, I've even cauterized knife wounds. In the field, you do what you have to do, and you keep going."

The words of a soldier. But they weren't looking for a soldier. They were looking for a killer.

Or are we looking for both?

The whir of the snowplow was louder.

"The sheriff will be coming for us," Thomas said. "We'll talk to Jenny and get her to describe the man who took her." He glanced up at the now-clear sky. "And we'll talk to Mercer. Find out what the EOD has learned about those victims."

Before they did… "We need to talk first," she said as she gave a determined nod.

His gaze instantly became shuttered.

"No more secrets, no more lies."

He flinched at that. "I haven't lied to you."

It almost seemed surreal to have this conversation with him. After everything that had happened the night before, they should have been close. Heck, it didn't get much closer than being someone's lover. But there was a wall between them.

Secrets.

And, yes, despite what he'd just said...lies.

"I want to know everything." They were alone. Now was the time to put it all out on the table. "From the moment that you saw me— running in those woods—until the moment you left me tied in that cabin." Because, yes, that part was obvious. She'd been left there with a dead man.

The sound of the plow grew louder. They'd tried to call the sheriff earlier, but they still had no service in the area. While they had a few more precious moments of privacy, she needed to hear the rest of Thomas's tale.

Even though part of her was almost afraid to hear what he had to say.

Hiding from the truth won't do any good.

"You heard me screaming in the woods, and you found me." She looked down at her wrists. "I'd been tied up, bound—"

"And he was hunting you."

Her head whipped up. Thomas wasn't looking at her. He was staring out at the snow.

"I knew what he was doing pretty quickly. Another hunter always knows…."

She shook her head, but he didn't see the movement.

"You were leaving a clear trail for him to follow. Broken branches, blood on the rocks. He expected to find you out there, but he didn't expect me." His voice was low and rough. "He jumped out of the bushes with a knife, and he went for your throat."

Her hand lifted to her throat. "The man… the man found with me that day… *His* throat had been cut."

Now he did look at her. His eyes blazed with emotion. "I wasn't going to let him kill you. And, like I said, he expected you—" his right hand flexed near his side "—not me. I got that knife away from him, and he was the one who died."

Her breath rushed out. "All of that was in the woods? But—but his body was found in the cabin. *I* was found in the cabin."

He looked away from her. "I was working a case. Undercover. Domestic terrorists were in the area. I…I couldn't be found with you. I couldn't be caught up in an investigation about a missing teen girl and her dead abductor."

"You left me." Saying the words...hurt. Her hand lowered to her chest and rubbed over the ache there.

"Yes," his voice was soft. "I left you. You kept trying to follow me, so I had to tie you up. I couldn't have you walking from one danger straight into another."

The pain in her chest seemed to get worse. "You were following orders." Mercer's orders. She'd thought Mercer was her friend. They'd met years before when she first joined the FBI. He'd taken an interest in her. Her supervisor had been in awe of the guy, and even though she hadn't realized quite how powerful Mercer was, Noelle had known he was a man who could help her.

Only he'd actually been the man hiding her past from her.

The pain of betrayal was there, and she wondered if it always would be.

"That's what a soldier does." Anger roughened Thomas's words. "And, yes, damn it, that was what I did." He swung to face her. "I took you to that cabin. I...called in backup."

"Mercer..."

"EOD agents put the body inside."

She'd gone over the reports. There hadn't been enough of the dead man's blood in the cabin, so the police had thought his body had been dumped there, but they'd never been able to find the kill site.

The EOD were too good at covering their tracks.

"I didn't want to tie you up. Your wrists were already raw and bloody."

She blinked away tears.

"You wouldn't stay behind. You kept trying to follow," he said quietly. "I didn't…I didn't have a choice."

"Actually, you did. You've known this for years, you could've said—"

"Before I left you at that cabin, I told you that you couldn't speak to the police about me. I told you I was working a case and lives were on the line." He yanked a hand through his hair. "At first, I thought you *were* covering for me. Doing what I'd asked because you promised me that you'd keep quiet."

She frowned at him.

"Later…later I realized you just didn't remember, and by then, I was in so deep at the EOD that telling you the real truth wasn't an option." His hand dropped. "I even thought it might be better for you. Not knowing. You seemed to be making a good life for yourself. You graduated at the top of your college class. You went to Quantico. You had a wide circle of friends. Hell, you were even involved with that jerk psychology professor for a time."

She took a step back as realization slammed into her. "You were watching me." That was her gut response. He wasn't just quoting facts he'd discovered in some background report on her. The anger that hummed in his voice when he talked about her ex, Jim…it was too strong. Too personal.

He'd even told her before that he'd seen her, but she hadn't seen him.

Because he was watching me?

"I needed to make sure you were all right."

The growl of an engine grew louder. A snow-plow? The sheriff? She didn't look away from Thomas to find out. "How long have you been watching me?"

"It's not… I check on you, okay? When I'm back in the U.S. Between assignments." He seemed to be weighing his words and respond-ing so carefully. "I just like to make sure that you're safe."

I'll always be with you.

"The EOD gathered a lot of intel on your attacker, and we thought it was just one guy, working alone. You seemed to be the first vic-tim he'd taken. Mercer believed that, with his death, it was over, but I…just needed to be sure." He sighed. "I needed to be sure because at night, when I closed my eyes, I would still hear you screaming for me to help you."

There it was. All of the secrets from her past. The truth she'd sought for so long, and now, hearing all of those details just made her feel numb. Like she'd just taken a dive into another ice pond.

But it made sense. His story explained the strange connection she'd felt with Thomas. The awareness. He *was* her past. The man who'd saved her in the dark.

He saved me, then left me.

No wonder her emotions had been all over the place with him.

She'd even…even wondered if she might be falling for him.

"Say something," he gritted out, his eyes glinting.

"What do you want me to say?" That emotionless voice didn't sound right. It didn't sound like her voice at all.

"Yell at me. Curse me. Tell me I'm a jerk for keeping the truth from you." He took another step toward her. "Tell me that I should've chosen you and turned my back on the EOD."

Her eyes widened. "Is that what you want me to say?" As she stared into Thomas's eyes, Noelle saw his guilt. Heavy. Thick.

"You were seventeen." Another step brought

him even closer. "You were terrified. You… you asked me to stay with you. You begged me to stay."

She shook her head. The memory was right there. "And you said you'd always be with me."

"I'm sorry," he rasped.

So was she.

The growling of that engine was so close. She rushed away from the window and yanked open the front door. Noelle saw not one but two vehicles driving up behind the snowplow. One was the sheriff's car and the other, a dark SUV. As she watched, they braked and the passenger door of the SUV opened. A man jumped out. Her eyes narrowed as she stared at him.

He wore a thick coat, but she could tell his shoulders were broad. His back was straight. He yanked off his woolen cap as he headed toward her. The closer he came, the more she noticed the gray at his temples, his stony visage….

"No way," Noelle whispered. Sunglasses shielded the man's eyes, but she knew they would be green—and sharp.

Another man flanked the guy, a man who walked with a tense alertness, which broadcasted his military background.

She knew the second guy was a bodyguard,

even before he turned and blocked the sheriff from heading up to the cabin.

And the man striding so confidently toward them was none other than—

"Mercer?" Thomas said, shock in his voice.

He should be shocked. As a rule, the EOD boss didn't do field work. He stayed in his office, and he pulled the strings. But, thanks to the recent attack at the EOD, there *was* no D.C. office.

"Inside," Bruce Mercer snapped. "You never know who's watching."

He was the man who'd kept her past from her. The man who knew where all the bodies were buried in D.C.

And because he was there, right in front of her, Noelle knew the situation in Camden, Alaska, had to be very, very bad.

If Bruce Mercer was there, then death wasn't far behind.

Chapter Eight

"Judging by the way Noelle is looking at me, I guess you told her everything, Agent Anthony?"

They were inside the cabin. Mercer was pacing near the fireplace while the man he'd brought with him—Thomas easily recognized Aaron Black—stood guard near the door.

For Aaron to be there, *with* Mercer, Thomas knew the situation had to be serious. He'd worked with the ex-SEAL before on cases that didn't involve hostage rescue. They'd involved cleanup.

Target disposal.

Death.

"*You* should've told me the truth," Noelle said, voice sharp. "As soon as I came on with the EOD. You should've—"

"I thought the past was dead and buried. Part of it was dead." Mercer waved toward Thomas. "Thanks to Agent Anthony."

His back teeth locked. Mercer wasn't exactly helping the situation.

"We thought the man who'd taken you—"

"Justin Hardin," Noelle bit out. "His name was Justin Hardin."

Mercer would know that. The man knew everything.

"We thought he was working alone. Our intel was wrong. We didn't realize just how mistaken we'd been until you uncovered those photographs at the senator's place."

Now he understood why Mercer was in Camden. "You identified those girls."

"Yes." Mercer turned sharply on his heel and faced Noelle. "They were taken from different states. Two even from different countries, *before* you went missing. The geographical area was so wide that we never connected the dots together." He exhaled. "That was a mistake that we have remedied now."

Noelle's arms were crossed over her chest. "Those girls were all taken that long ago? Then they—"

"I don't believe any of those girls are still alive."

Noelle's shoulders sagged.

Thomas narrowed his gaze on Mercer. "Since when does the EOD get involved on a serial's crime?" They didn't, not unless…

"The girls were taken from different states and different countries." It was Aaron who spoke. His voice was low and devoid of accent. "The techs at the EOD matched all of those abductions with ports of call that Senator Lawrence Duncan visited while he was enlisted in the navy."

Noelle shook her head. "He didn't do this! He's dead, and Jenny Tucker was abducted *after* Duncan's body had already been found. Her mother saw her leave the house that morning, and we know Duncan was killed during the night."

"Our mistake before," Mercer said, cutting through her words but sending a sympathetic glance her way, or at least, as sympathetic as Mercer got, "was thinking there was only one killer involved. Obviously, there were two."

Red flashed on Noelle's high cheekbones. "Justin Hardin is *dead*."

"Hardin was hunting you," Aaron said. His gaze slid to Thomas. "We, um, learned that from Agent Anthony. He was the man after you in those Alabama woods."

He wanted to cross to Noelle's side. This situation was so messed up.

"But Hardin had a partner." Aaron's head inclined toward Noelle. "One we missed."

"You're *still* missing the truth!" The red

grew darker on her cheeks. "If there was a second killer, there would be more victims." She pointed at Mercer. "You said the girls were all taken before me. The killer wouldn't just stop after my abduction. He wouldn't simply *quit* killing. It doesn't work like that. Killing would be a compulsion for him. He'd keep taking victims because he *had* to. If we're dealing with a serial, he'd have a ritual that he followed and—" Noelle broke off as her eyes widened. "Hunting."

"Yes," Mercer said softly.

Thomas was lost. His stare drifted between Mercer and Noelle. What was he missing?

"He kept killing, but he changed his prey." Noelle's gaze seemed unfocused, and Thomas knew she was trying to profile the man they were after. "He was hunting girls before, teenagers, but... Something changed."

"Maybe the fact that his partner died?" Aaron tossed out. "Maybe that sent the guy into a tailspin."

Noelle rubbed her temples. "He's hunting. Last night, when he lured Thomas and me outside of this place, he was *hunting* us."

Mercer frowned. "He was here? What the hell? Why didn't you say something sooner?"

Because they hadn't exactly had the chance. Thomas locked gazes with the director. "We pursued him in the storm last night. Noelle shot him, but he got away."

"He got away because of me." Noelle's chin came up. "The attacker threw me onto weak ice and I fell through. Thomas had to pull me to safety."

Aaron lifted a brow. "Uh, you went through the ice?"

"I survived." Her voice was cold. Noelle started to pace. "He's a hunter, and he knows this area." Noelle's gaze snapped toward Thomas. "He started by hunting girls—they both did—but... After the partner died, maybe our guy realized he needed more of a challenge. He had to go for tougher game."

"And that's precisely what he did." Mercer nodded grimly. "I got Sydney to pull up every piece of intel we had on the late Senator Duncan."

Thomas knew Mercer was referring to Sydney Ortez. The woman was a genius with computers and information retrieval.

Mercer continued, "It seems that the senator's enemies—a few in the U.S. but particularly abroad—had a tendency to vanish."

"They were hunted," Thomas surmised. "By the senator?"

Mercer hesitated.

"He didn't get his hands dirty," Noelle said,

and her words sounded so certain. "Not in the attack in D.C. and not when we were pushed off the road that first night. Duncan was a background guy. A puppeteer…"

Just like Mercer?

"He had others do the bloody work for him," Aaron said. His hands were loose at his sides.

"Yes." Noelle licked her lips. "If the earlier abductions all matched up with the senator's ports, then Duncan probably knew the killer. He knew what he was doing."

Of course, the senator wouldn't have stopped the killer.

"I was looking at it all wrong." Noelle kept pacing. "I thought the pictures we discovered at the senator's place were trophies. Mementos to remind Duncan of the victims, but they weren't."

"So what the hell were they?" Aaron asked. His blue eyes were narrowed and his jaw was locked.

Noelle stopped pacing. "They were blackmail material. He knew the killer's identity, and Duncan used those images to get the killer to do *his* dirty work."

"Like an attack dog on a leash." Thomas saw the situation perfectly now. "But if that's true, then something in those photos should tell us our killer's identity."

Mercer nodded. "And that's where Noelle comes in." He advanced toward her. "You're the one who can figure this one out. You're the one who can put the pieces of this puzzle together and help us determine just who this sick bozo is before he has the chance to hurt anyone else."

HE WAS STILL bleeding and he was getting weaker by the moment. The bullet was lodged in him. He had to get it out, but every time he tried to get a hold on the thing, he just made the wound bigger. Deeper.

The snowplows were out, clearing the little town of Camden. He was in the shadows because that was his custom. He'd spent most of his life hiding, one way or another.

When you had a monster inside, you had to be careful. If the world saw you for what you really were, they'd destroy you.

His father had told him that. His father had seen him for exactly what he was. His old man had hoped the military would change him. Focus him. And, in a way, it had.

Because in the navy, he'd met Lawrence Duncan.

He watched as a bundled woman made her way to the small pharmacy in town. Figured that place would open first.

He would've preferred to find a veterinarian or some kind of doc, but the pharmacy tech would have to do. There wasn't anyone else who could help him, not now.

He made his way across the street. Saw the blood that dripped from him and splattered down in the snow. He should clean up his trail. But…

Too weak.

He pushed open the pharmacy door. The lights weren't on. Power wasn't back on in the town. He'd tried to use a phone before, but he hadn't been able to connect. The storm had knocked all communication down.

"We're not quite open yet!" A cheery voice called out. "Give me just a few minutes, and I'll help you."

He pulled his knife from its sheath. He walked down the narrow aisle. Saw the woman as she shrugged out of her coat. She was built like Noelle, long, slender, almost delicate lines. But her hair was a dark black, not a red.

"Be with you soon!" She said, not glancing back.

Her mistake.

He grabbed her and put the knife to her throat as he jerked her back against his chest. "You'll be with me right now." He had a ski mask over his face, so he twisted her around toward him, all the while keeping that knife right at her throat.

"Please…" she whispered.

He shook his head. "I'm not planning to kill you." Not yet, anyway. "Because you're going to help me, aren't you?"

The knife cut into her neck.

And she nodded.

"JENNY…" NOELLE KEPT her voice low and gentle. She didn't want to upset Jenny. The girl had already been through enough.

She was at Jenny's house. Jenny's mother was behind the girl, pacing nervously, and the sheriff watched from a position near the door.

"We need to take her over to Harrison County Medical," the sheriff said, voice tight. "Get her thoroughly checked out and—"

"No!" Jenny's desperate cry seemed to echo in Noelle's ears. Jenny glanced over her shoulder. "Mom, you promised I wouldn't have to go anywhere! I don't want— I need to stay here!"

Jenny's mother caught her daughter's hand and held tight. "You're not going anywhere."

The sheriff growled.

Noelle squared her shoulders. "I know the officers collected your clothing last night."

"Evidence," Jenny whispered as her gaze dropped down to her lap. "They said it was evidence. They—they sent me back home in borrowed clothes this morning."

Noelle glanced toward Jenny's mother.

"The storm trapped us at the sheriff's station. That's as far as the ambulance could get in that weather." Her gaze cut to Hodges. "But my girl is fine now. She doesn't need a hospital." Her breath heaved out as she pointed at the sheriff. "And he asked us questions all night, so I don't see why we have to answer any more now!"

"I promise, this won't take long." Noelle saw Jenny flinch. She wanted to reach out and touch the girl, offer comfort, but Jenny seemed frozen before her. "I need you to describe the man who took you."

"I *did* already!" Jenny's voice broke a bit. "I told the sheriff...he was tall, wide shoulders. He had dark hair and stubble on his face."

"Caucasian, African-American—"

"Caucasian," Jenny whispered.

"Were there any marks on his face? Any scars or tattoos that you noticed?"

Jenny shook her head.

"What about his eyes? What color were they?"

"Brown. I think they were brown."

"Good, Jenny. You're doing really, really well." Noelle knew interrogations with victims had to be handled carefully. If you pushed too hard, victims could break. If you didn't push hard enough, they might not be able to tell important details. "When he spoke to you, did the man have any accent?"

Another shake of Jenny's head was her answer.

Okay. Time to try a different tactic because, unfortunately, the man Jenny had just described could be *anyone*. "When we found you in the cabin, you were screaming."

A tear leaked down Jenny's cheek. "He told me that I had to scream."

"Because he wanted—"

"He wanted you to die." Jenny glanced up at her. "You're Noelle, and he said you had to die."

Chill bumps rose on Noelle's skin. "He mentioned me by name?"

"Yes."

"What did he say?"

"I wasn't…good enough. But you—you would be more fun. So I had to scream so he could see you. He said…he said he just wanted to see you."

No, he'd wanted to kill her. He'd wanted to kill them all.

"He told me that he liked to see his girls."

The photos. "Did he take any pictures of you while you were in that cabin?"

"Yes." Shame burned in that word. "I was

crying and begging him, and he was taking my picture. He was...filming me with his phone."

Because the sicko didn't use a Polaroid any longer, but he still needed the memories of his victims.

"This is very important." Noelle leaned toward Jenny. "Did you ever hear him talking with anyone else? Did you *see* anyone else with him?"

Jenny bit her lower lip. "I don't...I don't think so."

"Are you sure, Jenny?" Because the man had worked with a partner years before. Maybe he was up to his old tricks. Two hunters.

A game? A competition?

"I only heard him. No one else."

Noelle smiled at her. "Thank you, Jenny. You've been very helpful." She rose from the couch and turned for the door.

Jenny grabbed her hand. "When am I going to stop seeing him?"

Noelle stilled. Then, slowly, her gaze slid to find Jenny's.

"Every time I close my eyes, he's there." Jenny swallowed and the little click of sound was almost painful to hear. "When will that stop? When will he get out of my mind?"

"When I catch him and lock him in a cell.

Then you won't ever have to worry about seeing him again."

Jenny nodded and she let go of Noelle.

"Thank you for your time." Noelle inclined her head to Jenny and Jenny's mother. Then she left because looking at Jenny was far too much like looking at herself.

The sheriff followed her out. Noelle had been given a new coat from the sheriff's department, one that fit better, and it helped to block the chill in the air.

The door shut behind them. "I need to head back to the station," Noelle said. Thomas and Aaron were out running down leads and searching the area. They thought if the perp was looking for medical aid, he might be staying close to the town—and they were determined to find him.

When the sheriff didn't speak, Noelle glanced his way. He was watching her with a hooded gaze. "Sheriff?"

"Locking him up won't stop that girl's nightmares." His hand rasped over his stubble-covered jaw. "You and I both know that, don't we?"

Her head tilted as she studied him.

"Camden was a quiet town before all this mess started." His lips pressed together and formed a grim line. "But Los Angeles, well, it had more than its share of crime."

So there was more to the sheriff than met the eye. Wasn't that the story with everyone? "You came up here to get away."

"I got tired of arriving too late."

She knew exactly what that was like.

"You're not FBI."

Noelle didn't so much as blink. "My ID says otherwise."

He laughed, but the sound was grim. "This ain't my first rodeo, and I know FBI agents when I see them. They're stiff, by the book, and they sure as hell don't race through fire without so much as twitching." He pointed at her. "It was the other agent who gave things away. Military. Covert, I'm betting."

"The past few days have been very stressful," she said carefully. "I think—"

"That bigwig who flew in on his *own* chopper, he isn't FBI. I don't know what organization you all work for, but I do need to know this." He exhaled on a rough breath. "Is my town safe? Or will more people be hurt soon?"

Watch what you say. "We are going to catch the man who's behind Jenny's abduction."

"Yeah, but are you and that team of yours going to do it before or *after* I have to clean up more bodies?"

THE SNOW WAS RED.

Thomas stopped instantly when he caught sight of the red drops. He lifted his hand, an old habit, as he signaled to Aaron.

Aaron bent low and gazed at the blood and at the faint trail that led across the street. The trail ended right at the door of an old pharmacy.

The lights were out in that pharmacy. Odd, since power had come back to the city an hour ago.

"Cover me," Thomas said flatly. He advanced toward the building, aware of Aaron following him. Thomas had his gun out, and he was more than ready to use it on the man who'd nearly killed Noelle the night before.

There were more droplets at the door, as if the guy had paused for a moment before he'd gone inside. Thomas reached for the knob. It twisted easily in his grasp. He shoved open that door and rushed inside.

Aaron was right on his heels.

Drops of crimson dotted the aisle. He followed them, then saw the heavy, blood-soaked cloths on the counter.

A quick search showed no one was in the pharmacy. The back door was unlocked. Just like the front.

"Looks like the guy got away again." Aaron shook his head. "But we had to be close."

Thomas studied the discarded bandages—and the bullet that had been left behind.

"He dug it out, huh?" Aaron whistled. "I had to do that once. Thought I'd pass out before the bullet came out of my stomach."

Thomas's gaze swept the scene once more. "He didn't dig it out himself." That just made things so much worse.

"What? How do you know?"

Thomas grabbed the purse that had fallen on the ground near the red-stained counter.

"Hell," Aaron muttered.

Thomas pulled out the ID inside. Sarah Finway. A Sarah Finway who was most definitely *not* there any longer.

"He's got another victim," Thomas said.

NOELLE STARED AT the photos on the wall. All of those girls. Scared. Blindfolded. So alone.

But you weren't really alone, were you? Because their abductor had been the one to take the photos.

"I've got more men coming in," Mercer said.

She nearly jumped at his voice. She'd been so intent on those girls Noelle hadn't even heard him enter the little office.

"They'll be here in two hours."

Right. When Mercer said jump, people flew.

"They'll search every inch of the senator's

house, and if there's more evidence to find," he nodded and said, "we'll have it."

Her phone rang. Noelle glanced down, saw it was Thomas, and she answered immediately. "Did you find him?"

"He's got another victim."

Her fingers tightened around the instrument.

"A woman who worked at the pharmacy, Sarah Finway. The guy's blood is here, but he's not and neither is she."

Her heart thundered in her chest. "We can use his blood for DNA. If he's in the system, we'll have an ID."

"But we won't have *her*." Frustration boiled in Thomas's voice. "The guy knows this area. He'll stash her, and then he'll kill her, all while we're running down DNA."

Thomas wasn't used to this part of the business. EOD agents were men and women of action. They didn't run DNA checks. They didn't stalk after criminals. They went in. They attacked. They completed their missions.

And Thomas was right. By the time they got a DNA hit on the perp, Sarah Finway could be dead.

"I'm going to keep searching with Aaron. If we find anything, I'll call you."

"He knows this area. Be careful because you don't want to walk into another of his traps."

"I want to find the guy," Thomas fired back. "If he wants to hunt someone, if that's the way he likes to play, then he needs to come hunt me, not some innocent civilian."

When the call ended, Noelle kept holding the phone and staring at those pictures. "I need to talk with the sheriff," she said, not looking over her shoulder at Mercer. "And then I want to head back to the senator's place and talk with Paula Quill." Because Paula had been the senator's confidant. If there had been someone in and out of the senator's life for the past fifteen years, then Paula should know.

Mercer's footsteps padded out of the office. She knew he'd pull the sheriff in, one way or another. No one said no to Mercer. At least, not for long.

She put the phone down on the desk and let her gaze trek from image to image. They'd gotten names for the girls. Dates of their disappearances. She'd put the images in order based on those dates, and her focus shifted to the first girl who'd vanished.

Emma Jane Rogers. Age sixteen. She'd lived in Charleston.

"The first kill is the one that matters most," Noelle whispered as she leaned toward the image. There had to be something in the picture that could help her. Why had the killer begun with Emma Jane? Why her?

Had all of the others girls been taken because they *looked* like Emma?

Her finger pressed against the photograph. Emma Jane was wearing a necklace. They'd blown up the photo, and Noelle could see it appeared to be half of a heart. The kind of necklace young couples often wore. The girl would have one part, and the boy would have the other.

There were two images of Emma Jane. In one of the images, that necklace around her neck was clear.

In the other image, it was gone. Blood dripped over her neck, as if she'd been sliced with a knife.

As if someone had sliced the necklace off her?

Noelle quickly checked the other snapshots. None of the others were wearing any sort of jewelry. Their necks also didn't show any signs of having been cut. There were no injuries on those girls in the other photos at all.

These are the before shots.

Were there after shots someplace? Images that showed what had happened to the girls after the hunt was complete?

Noelle knew that there must be.

"Here's the sheriff."

Noelle turned at Mercer's flat words. He had a tight grip on the sheriff's arm. Hodges was glaring at him.

"I was in the middle of a briefing with my men!" Hodges sputtered. "You don't just drag a sheriff away—"

Mercer laughed. "I drag anyone away." He pointed toward Noelle. "Now, answer her questions because if anyone can figure out this guy, it's her."

She already had puzzle pieces flying through her mind. "He's a local, Sheriff. Someone who knows this area extremely well. He'd keep to himself. He's a male…probably in his late thirties, close to Senator Duncan's age. He's ex-navy, so he might be sporting some tattoos that he got during the service."

Hodges shook his head. "This is a town of barely a thousand people. I know everyone."

"And that's why you know *him*. He might come in and out, drifting in when Senator Duncan is in the area. He won't stay all year, but he *knows this place.* He'd be the best hunter in the area. He'd have to be. So think of someone who's gone after big game. Someone who—"

The sheriff stiffened.

"You know who it is," Mercer growled.

"There *is* a guy like that. His name's Patrick,

Patrick Porter." Hodges shook his head. "He's the best hunter in the area. He comes through the area because he likes to go after bears." His gaze darted to the photos on the wall. "Lot of hunters come through here because they want to go after the big game, but Porter... He comes back each year. And he always gets his prey."

Her heart raced in her chest. "Is he here now?"

"I don't know." Hodges ran a hand over his face. "But he usually stays at the old Burrows cabin. It's about four miles north of the senator's place."

A perfect fit.

"Get your men out there," Mercer snapped. "Now."

Noelle yanked out her phone as the sheriff rushed away. She had Thomas back on the line seconds later. "We have a target. His name's Patrick Porter, and the sheriff said he's at a cabin about four miles north of the senator's home." That would sure put the guy in close enough proximity to kill. "The sheriff is heading there now."

"You know he probably has a few cabins out there, Noelle," Thomas said. "Places to hide his victims."

Yes, she knew that. "But he might have left us something we could use at the Burrows place."

Or maybe the guy wasn't thinking clearly because of his injuries. She'd seen plenty of perps slip up over the years. "Get back to the station, and we'll go after him with the sheriff." Because she planned to be on the scene.

She pushed the phone into her pocket and spun back around. She marched for the door, but Mercer put up his hand, blocking her. "You need to be careful."

His words had her pausing. Since when did the EOD director worry his agents couldn't do their jobs?

Her eyes narrowed on him. "I might not have military experience, but I survived just fine as an FBI agent. If you don't think I can do this, then you never should've brought me on the team."

"I know you can do any job." He shut the door, sealing them inside.

Noelle gave a frantic shake of her head. "Thomas is on his way. I need to get directions for that cabin. I should—"

"Thomas briefed me on what happened last night."

For an instant, her cheeks burned. No *way* was he talking about what she suspected. There were sure some things the boss didn't need to know.

"You nearly died. If you'd been alone, do you think you would have made it out of that water?"

"You might be surprised," Noelle said as she lifted her chin. "I'm a lot stronger than you give me credit for being."

He laughed at that, the sound low and rough. "Oh, I know you're plenty strong. All of my agents are. I didn't keep the truth from you because I thought you were weak." His head tilted. "Is that what you think?"

She didn't know what to think.

"You changed Thomas on that mission. He was still young, a new agent, but he was focused totally on the job. Until you. He tried to go back for you—twice—even though we told him that you'd been taken in by the local cops."

Her lashes lowered to shield her eyes.

"He was undercover. He saved your life, but by staying on his mission, he saved the lives of hundreds of other people, too."

Noelle swallowed.

"Don't blame him. If you're furious, and you've got a right to be, blame me."

Her lashes lifted. "I do."

He nodded. "Fair enough."

She didn't see where a whole lot was fair right then. "I don't have time for this now. Sarah Finway is out there, and she needs help." She pushed past him and grabbed for the doorknob.

"That's why you're an EOD agent. Because you put others first. It's what our job is about. We have to give up the things that we want most, in order to get the mission accomplished."

There was a note of pain in his voice, which pulled at her. She glanced back.

"You didn't have the clearance to know about Thomas's actions. Not until you joined the EOD."

"That's why you pushed for me to join the division."

He inclined his head.

"And this particular mission? Did you know about the link to my past?" The guy seemed to know *everything,* while Noelle felt as if she were floundering around in the dark.

"I knew that Senator Duncan was connected to the destruction of the EOD office. I'd been recently looking into his past, and I was noticing connections that alarmed me. Enemies who were vanishing... I was putting all of those dots together and getting a picture of a man who was a national-security threat." His eyes narrowed. "I sent you on this mission because I knew you could figure him out. I paired you with Thomas...because I knew it was time for you to understand the past."

"You should have *told* me."

His eyes glinted. "Every day I make decisions that impact thousands of lives. The jobs my agents do… They're dangerous. They're deadly. They are jobs most people will never even know about." He heaved out a hard breath. "I have to make judgments. I do the best that I can." He backed away from her. "You're alive, Agent Evers, because one of my operatives saved your life. Now it's your job to save the lives of others."

Mercer had never seemed quite so human to her as he did in that moment. There was pain in his voice, and she'd caught the faint tremble of his hands.

"This case is personal to you," Noelle noted quietly.

"Senator Duncan almost took out dozens of agents who were in the EOD building. Damn straight it's personal." He pinned her with his stare. "So we're closing this case. We're bringing down this Patrick Porter. We're going to learn everything about him and his connection to Duncan. No one messes with my agents." His eyes sharpened on her. "Not any of them."

"LET ME GO," Sarah whispered as she sat in the old, wooden chair, her hands bound behind her back. "Please…I won't tell anyone about you."

They always said the same thing. Always made promises they couldn't keep.

It was the lies that got to him.

She'd lied to him. She'd started this whole chain of events.

"I helped you," Sarah said, the tears making her voice husky. Tears were so useless. He wished she'd stop shedding them. "I dug out the bullet. I sewed you up."

A twisted, tangled mess of stitches.

"Please," she said again. "Just let me go…I am *begging* you…"

Well, if she was going to beg…

"You aren't my usual type." These days, he went for a much bigger challenge. He used his knife to cut through her ropes. She rose to her feet, stumbling a bit. He motioned to the door. "Go."

She didn't move.

He rolled his eyes, then roared, *"Go!"*

She rushed for the door.

His hold tightened on the knife. "I'll give you a five-minute head start. Since you did help me…it's the least you deserve."

Her head jerked back toward him. Her eyes widened in horror.

He smiled. "You're wasting precious time."

Because after the hell he'd been through, he needed a hunt. Sarah wasn't his first choice, but she'd do. And she'd send a message to Noelle Evers.

I can kill whenever I want. He was the perfect killing machine. No one could stop him. No one would stop him.

Sarah screamed as she ran into the wilderness. She wouldn't be screaming for long. He'd make sure of that.

He looked down at the blade. And he remembered another girl. A knife had sliced against her throat. She'd begged, too. Asked him to believe her. To trust her.

He'd also given her a chance to survive. But she hadn't run fast enough. They never did.

He waited, counting, then… "Time's up."

The thrill of the hunt heated his veins.

Chapter Nine

The sheriff's men had fanned out to search the area around the Burrows cabin. Thomas watched as those men made heavy paths in the snow. Aaron was behind him, and Noelle was at his side.

"It's too easy."

Noelle glanced over at his words. "You know he's not here," Thomas told her flatly. "He took her someplace else."

She started heading toward the cabin just as the sheriff appeared in the doorway. "Place is clear!" Hodges called out. "It looks like no one's been here all season!"

"Appearances can be deceiving," Thomas heard Noelle murmur as she kept walking toward the cabin.

"I'm betting the guy has half a dozen places he uses for hiding up here," Aaron said. His gun was holstered at his hip. "If the sheriff is right about him coming up for big game, then he'd have to know the area."

That was their problem. The man knew the area better than they did, and that was why he kept getting away. "He's not going to stay up here forever," Thomas said. "If we don't find him soon, he could slip away."

And take the answers they needed with him.

Noelle disappeared into the cabin.

The sheriff joined his men on the search.

Thomas had just taken a step forward when he heard the cry. Sharp and high. At first, he thought it was an animal. One that was hurt.

But then the cry came again, echoing up to him.

A scream.

Thomas whirled around. Aaron had already taken off, running toward the scream. Other deputies were scrambling to follow. "Be careful!" Thomas bellowed. "He likes his traps!" Thomas didn't doubt for an instant the man would use human bait to pull them into another one of his hunts.

He glanced back toward the cabin. Noelle had just run outside. Her eyes were wide and desperate as she hurried after him.

They both knew that scream belonged to

Sarah Finway, and the fact they didn't hear any other cries…

We're coming, Sarah. Just hold on.

HE LIKED THE way the snow turned red. That was always a bonus he got when he hunted in the colder climates. Sarah had gotten farther than he'd expected. Probably because she knew the area nearly as well as he did. She'd used some shortcuts that he just had to admire.

A gurgle came from her lips.

He wiped the knife on his coat. The blood smeared. "It's okay. You just stay here and try to breathe, nice and slow. That will help you survive longer." He needed her to live for a few more minutes. He put the knife in its sheath. Then he drew out his gun.

Her eyes widened. Another frantic gurgle broke from her lips.

"Shh…" He aimed the gun at her head.

Tears leaked from her eyes.

"This isn't for you. Don't worry." He'd heard the sound of those engines. They'd been coming closer as he hunted. If he hadn't taken Sarah down when he had, she just might have made it to safety.

Yes, she'd been much better prey than he'd expected. "This gun is for the ones coming to save you." Because he wasn't going out of this battle quietly. It was time everyone knew about him.

No more shadows. No more secrets.

He already knew Jenny had spent the night at the sheriff's station. The storm had kept her there, so she would've had the whole night to talk about him—to tell the authorities what he looked like.

So he figured he had two choices—keep running…or go out fighting. Go out by showing them all *exactly* who they were dealing with in this battle.

For years, no one had known of his existence.

Soon, no one would ever forget him.

He just wished he had his rifle with him, but the handgun would have to do. He slipped back into the shadows cast by the snow-covered trees, and he waited.

"Sarah Finway!" Sheriff Hodges called as he raced to keep up with the pack searching for Sarah. *"Sarah!"*

Thomas saw the sheriff had his gun out, and Hodges was sweeping to the left and the right. They'd tracked that dying scream out here, but there was no sound now.

Other than the frantic cries from the sheriff and his deputies.

Aaron's shoulder brushed against Thomas's. "I don't like this." His voice was low.

Thomas didn't like this situation, either. They were surrounded by trees, so there were dozens of places for a perp to hide. The sheriff and his men were making enough noise to wake the dead.

"Footprints!" One of the deputies called out. "Here! I've got her!"

He had her *only* if those were Sarah's footprints.

Thomas's instincts screamed at him. Noelle started to follow the others. He grabbed her arm and barked out, "Stop!"

But it was too late. He heard the sharp thunder of gunfire. One blast. Two. Three.

Yells and screams filled the air.

"Damn it," Aaron growled. "It's like sheep to the slaughter!"

Thomas took cover, with Noelle right at his side. The deputies were firing back, but they seemed to be shooting wildly in all directions. They needed to calm down and focus.

"Where is he?" Thomas heard one deputy demand, voice breaking.

They didn't see their attacker, but they were still shooting?

"Stop firing!" Thomas shouted. He couldn't figure out anything with the chaos around him.

After a few moments, they did stop.

"The sheriff," Noelle whispered, horror in her voice.

Thomas peered around his cover. He cursed when he saw the sight before him. The sheriff was on the ground, a bloom of red on his body. And the woman—had to be Sarah Finway— she was just a few feet away from him.

It looked like the sheriff's chest was still rising and falling. Thomas wasn't so sure about Sarah.

Noelle lunged forward.

Thomas yanked her right back.

"Let me go!" she fiercely fought his grip, but her voice was whisper soft. "I have to help them!"

"Don't you see what he's doing? The sick freak is using them as bait. He'll shoot whoever goes out there next."

"They need *help.*" She shook her head. "I can't stay here and watch them die! I won't!"

Thomas tightened his hold on her. He studied the sheriff's body, trying to figure out the angle of entry. The trajectory of the bullet. The wind.

His gaze darted to the right. To the trees located there. Higher land. Best elevation. Perfect hunting zone.

He motioned toward Aaron, indicating the target zone. Aaron slipped back and, keeping to cover, began to advance to the right.

"Thomas…he's *dying*."

Yes, the sheriff was, but Thomas couldn't let her die, too. None of the deputies were going to help because they were too worried about getting shot.

"Give me cover," Thomas growled to her. "To the northwest."

"What? Thomas, no, I meant for me—"

He was already gone. He rushed out, kept his body low and dove toward the sheriff.

Gunfire blasted right near his face, missing him by about two inches.

"No!" He heard Noelle scream. Then she was firing back, giving Thomas the cover he so desperately needed. He grabbed the sheriff's arm and pulled the guy toward the trees. The bullet had sunk into the sheriff's stomach, and he was bleeding heavily.

"Get him…" the sheriff wheezed. "Shoot the…S…O…B."

The woman was still lying out there. Sarah Finway. Thomas knew more bullets would fly his way, but he braced himself, lifted his gun and went back toward her.

Gunfire erupted. There was a rough, choked cry.

Thomas used his body to try and cover the woman, but Sarah—

She's gone.

He couldn't find her pulse.

"I've got him!"

Thomas's head whipped up at Aaron's yell. And, sure enough, Aaron was standing with a bloody man in front of him. Aaron's gun was at the guy's temple.

Thomas's gaze trekked over the man's face as stunned recognition flooded through him. *I know him.*

Noelle raced from her cover then. She didn't go toward the killer. She ran for the sheriff. She fell to her knees and tried to apply pressure to the wound.

The man Aaron held began to laugh. "You think this is the end?" Blood dripped down the side of his face. "You have no clue!"

Aaron's mouth twisted into a snarl, and he slammed his gun into the side of the man's head.

The killer fell, and that sick laughter stopped.

Thomas's attention jumped to Aaron.

The ex-SEAL shrugged. "What? I thought he was about to attack. Sounded like a threat to me." His shoulders straightened. "Besides, Mercer wants this man brought in...by any means necessary."

Mercer's favorite order. *Any means necessary.*

"We're losing him!" Noelle yelled.

Thomas glanced back. Two of the deputies were around Sarah. The others were standing nervously beside Noelle and peering worriedly at the sheriff.

"We have to carry him out of here!" She whirled toward Thomas. "Help me!"

Always. He rushed back to her side, but when he saw the sickly pallor in the sheriff's face, Thomas knew the odds weren't good for the man.

The memory of the perp's laughter drifted through Thomas's mind.

You think this is the end? You have no clue.

Hell. What would happen next?

SHE HAD BLOOD on her hands. Noelle stared down at her palms. Mercer had used his chopper to airlift the sheriff to the nearest hospital. She could still hear the *whoop-whoop* of the chopper's blades.

Sheriff Hodges had been alive when they lifted off. Gut wounds could be so tricky. Would he be able to hang on and live long enough to reach the hospital?

Noelle wasn't so sure.

"We did it," Aaron said as he watched the aircraft rise. "Chalk up another capture for the EOD."

She didn't share his enthusiasm. "We lost

Sarah Finway." She turned toward him. "And Sheriff Hodges will be very, very lucky if he survives."

"But Patrick Porter won't *ever* hurt anyone else again." Aaron nodded grimly. "We can be sure of that."

She needed to wash her hands. She needed to change clothes. She also needed to interrogate Patrick Porter. *I'm sure that's not his real name.* Patrick would be full of secrets.

Mercer and Thomas had secured the man in the sheriff's station. She knew Mercer would be transporting the guy out of the area at the first opportunity.

She wanted her answers before that transfer. She wanted to know everything.

Noelle marched toward the station. Aaron followed closely, but he didn't speak. There were deputies inside the station, just two men. The others had gone with the sheriff. Mercer's orders. She knew he just didn't want a big audience around for what would come.

Once inside the station, she headed toward the small bathroom first. Noelle washed the blood away and tried not to remember the desperate look in the sheriff's eyes.

Failed.

Noelle knew that desperation would haunt her for the rest of her days.

A knock sounded on the bathroom door. "Noelle?" Thomas's voice called. "I've got fresh clothes for you."

She opened the door.

"Courtesy of Mercer," he said as he lifted a bag toward her.

Right. Mercer the Magic Man. He could do anything. She took the clothes from him and started to shut the door. Thomas's hand flew out, stopping her.

"He's going to try messing with your head." The words were a grim warning.

"I already know that." She was used to killers and their mind games. Finally, an area that was her specialty.

"Don't believe him. Don't believe the lies he's going to tell. Don't trust him."

Her head tilted. There was an odd note in his voice that made her nervous. "I know killers, Thomas. So that means I'm used to their lies." Some killers could lie so perfectly. They'd fool lie detectors. Fool law enforcement. Deceive everyone.

But she was ready for what was coming. Noelle didn't need Thomas to warn her.

"Mercer says…he wants to start the interrogation in five minutes. He's hoping to transfer the guy out by dawn."

That didn't give them a lot of time. "Mercer wants containment."

Thomas inclined his head. "He's already working on the cover-up."

Right. Because the world couldn't find out that a trusted senator had been bent on destruction—or that he'd been working side by side with a suspected serial killer.

Part of the EOD's job was to sweep away the dirty, dangerous secrets like this one.

Thomas's hand dropped. "I've always wanted to protect you."

She blinked at him.

"Remember that."

Then he was gone.

Her hands tightened around the bag. She couldn't shake the feeling there was more going on with this case. More… Something that had rattled even the normally controlled Thomas "Dragon" Anthony.

She changed quickly and made sure all of the blood was gone from her hands. Her fingers were trembling slightly, and she clenched them into fists as she drew in a steadying breath. The case wasn't over. Not yet. It wouldn't be over until they uncovered all of the secrets Patrick Porter possessed.

After another bracing breath, Noelle opened the door. She expected the narrow hallway to be empty. It wasn't. Thomas waited for her, with his back propped against the nearby wall.

"Thomas?"

He stared down at his hands. "I've done things in my life that I regret."

"We all do things that we regret."

His head lifted, and he gave her a sad smile. "I was trained to kill. Designed to be a perfect weapon. Trust me. There are things in my past better left forgotten."

Noelle cleared her throat. "Forgetting isn't all it's cracked up to be."

He straightened from the wall and reached for her. "Are you sure about that?"

His hold was strong, hard, and a bright intensity burned in his gaze.

"More of your past is going to come out, baby, and I need you to trust me."

Oh, but that did not sound good. "I do trust you."

"Enough to forgive what I've done?"

"Thomas…" He was scaring her.

His hand rose and curled under her chin. "I've watched you for so long that you seem like you're just a natural part of my life." His gaze searched hers. "But there are still secrets out there, and I don't want them to hurt you. I don't want *anything* to hurt you."

She felt as if she were missing something.

"I'll do what I must, in order to protect you."

She wasn't asking for protection.

His head bent, and Thomas pressed a kiss to her lips. He seemed to savor her. Almost helplessly, Noelle leaned toward him. After the madness of the past few days, Thomas was the only certain thing in her life.

When they touched, she needed.

When they kissed, she wanted.

He'd gotten past her guard when no other man had. Because of their shared past? Perhaps. But maybe it was just because he was... Thomas.

He let the kiss linger. She never wanted it to end. She wished they didn't have a killer waiting. She wanted to be with Thomas. To push away the fear and worry and simply *live*.

But he stepped back. "My first loyalty is to you. Remember that."

She could still taste him.

"From here on out, it always will be." He turned away from her and marched down the hall.

Noelle realized her fingers were trembling again, and a chill had slid down her spine. It was strange. Thomas's words had sounded like a warning.

But what else did he need to protect her from?

THE LITTLE SHERIFF'S station in Camden didn't have any interrogation rooms, but the place did sport two cells. And Patrick Porter was currently pacing the floor in one of those narrow cells.

When Noelle started walking toward him, he immediately stopped that pacing. His head snapped up, and he smiled at her.

She heard Thomas growl behind her.

She and Thomas were the only two conducting this interrogation. Mercer had gotten Aaron to install a video camera, and the feed was going back to him. Mercer wouldn't be making a personal appearance for this questioning period, though, not unless he absolutely needed to do so. Noelle knew when it came to EOD prisoners, Mercer had a policy of standing back.

Because he'd been burned too many times before.

"Did the sheriff die?" Patrick didn't sound particularly concerned about that possibility. Actually, he was more gleeful.

Noelle shook her head. "He's stable." At least, that was what she'd been told moments before. "He's on his way to the hospital. Your bullet missed its mark."

The glee faded as the faint lines near his eyes tightened. "I don't miss my mark."

"You did this time." She nodded toward him. Blood had broken through on his shirt. "Maybe the wound I gave you made you weak."

He laughed. "Nothing makes me weak." His gaze slid to Thomas. "Bet you can't say the same."

Thomas didn't say anything.

"We want to know where the bodies are," Noelle said softly. "That's the only reason we're talking to you right now. We know about all of the victims, starting with Emma Jane in Charleston."

"You have no clue about my victims." Disgust laced the words.

"We found your photographs. We saw the girls—"

Patrick laughed. She truly hated the sound of his grating laughter. His eyes were still on Thomas, but they were starting to fill with what looked like…recognition? "I'll be damned," the killer said as he advanced toward the bars. "It really is you…and she has no clue, does she? *Dragon*."

Thomas still wasn't speaking.

Patrick's fingers curled around the bars. "Your hair's shorter. Your face is harder. Looks like you broke your nose a few times over the years." He laughed. "They've got *you* in here? Don't they know what you've done?" His gaze came back to Noelle. "What he did to *you*."

When they'd been in that hallway, Thomas sure hadn't mentioned he knew the suspect. But then, he'd been busy kissing her. Noelle's heart was galloping in her chest, but she didn't let her expression alter. *Dragon.* The guy could've learned of Thomas's moniker in a dozen ways. He could just be playing with them now.

"I want to know where those girls are," Noelle said again.

Patrick's hold tightened around the bars. "Get the Dragon here to tell you."

A knot of tension formed at the nape of her neck. *Push him. Don't let him get to you.* "I know you were involved with Emma Jane. She was your girl, right? And she tried to leave you."

Now, *that* got his gaze flying toward her. "You don't know a damn thing about Emma!"

"I know that you two had matching necklaces. Hearts. You gave one half of the heart to her, and you wore its mate. When she betrayed you, well, that was when you snapped. You kidnapped her. You tortured her. Then you killed her."

Silence.

Patrick rested his forehead against the bars. "Every killer starts somewhere, right, Dragon?"

She didn't like the way the guy kept baiting Thomas. Worse, she didn't like the ice that kept growing in her gut. Ice that told Noelle she was missing something. Something very, very important.

"Are all the girls dead?" She stepped a bit closer to the cell. Not too close, though, because she didn't want him to be able to grab her. "Senator Duncan had pictures of them in his shed, but they were *your* pictures, weren't they? Pictures you'd taken to remind you of the kills."

"Duncan is dead," Patrick murmured. "And he never even saw the attack coming."

Beside her, Thomas shifted his stance, a ripple of movement that seemed menacing.

"Duncan thought he could control me, but I got tired of playing by his rules." Patrick's stare, a bright, glinting blue, raked over her. Dark stubble lined his jaw and his skin was a deep gold. "Especially when he sent me after you."

She stared back into those blue eyes and knew she was staring straight at evil.

"I remember you. I never forgot you." His head lifted from the bars as he laughed. "Dragon, there, he killed the wrong man. Did you know that? Justin Hardin wasn't the one hunting you. He was just the one to keep you in that cabin. You fought him, though, and you got away. You ran. Justin wasn't good at hunting, not like me. He called me, said he was going after you. Promised he'd have you waiting for me..."

"I wasn't waiting," Noelle snapped out as more pieces from her past slid into place.

"Because the Dragon killed Justin." He shook his head and focused on Thomas once more. "Did you do it to protect the girl...or because you didn't want Justin telling what he knew about you?"

Noelle rocked forward onto the balls of her feet. "How about you tell me how those pictures wound up with Senator Duncan, or maybe... maybe you want me to guess on that? Because I've got some ideas..."

Patrick shrugged. "Then let's hear them."

"You were stationed together with Duncan in the navy." They had EOD agents pulling up the senator's enlistment records. "I bet you kept those photos close, because you'd need them close." Looking at them would've been a compulsion. "But if you were bunking with Duncan, he would've had access to your area. I think he found them, only, instead of turning you in, he kept the photos so that he could blackmail you."

Patrick gave a low whistle. "You're only half right."

She didn't like the coldness in his stare. The man was in total control. She needed to rattle his cage and make that control shatter. "You were going after girls then…" Time to press for more. Time to *shatter*. "But after your enlistment, after you started fighting and killing in battle, did you think they were too easy? You're the big game hunter. And they weren't big enough game."

His gaze drifted dismissively over her. "No, you weren't."

Thomas stepped forward.

"The girls—you—were expendable. Weak. They all cried and begged too quickly. Some didn't even have the sense to run. I mean, hell, everyone is supposed to have a survival instinct, right? Isn't that what the experts say?"

She didn't respond.

"But they didn't. They died easily."

She studied him carefully. There was no emotion in his voice. No remorse. No glee. He was simply stating a fact. She'd wondered before if he were a psychopath. She wasn't wondering any longer. "Why didn't Duncan turn you in?"

But she knew…

Noelle didn't like the sardonic little smile curling Patrick's thin lips. "Most people would've turned me in. I mean, that would be the *right* thing to do, huh? That's what you think, don't you, *Noelle?*"

From the corner of her eye, Noelle saw Thomas clench his hands into fists.

"But Duncan wasn't like most folks. He was like me."

One psychopath, finding another.

"He kept the photos and told me he'd turn me in unless I did a job for him. Someone had made him very, very angry, you see, and he wanted that person eliminated."

"Then he should've done the job himself." This tight snarl came from Thomas.

Patrick shrugged. "Not his way. He gave me the prey, and he told me to hunt. I did."

Mercer's suspicions had been right. This guy had become Lawrence's attack dog.

"I found out I liked my new prey. They fought harder. They made me have to work for the rush."

The rush he'd first got when he killed Emma Jane. "Emma Jane was a crime of passion." Strange, when he was so passionless now. "Emma Jane was probably the only person you ever really connected with, and she betrayed you."

He lunged forward and grabbed the bars. "I was eighteen! I'd just enlisted. She couldn't even wait two months for me to come home. *Two. Months.*"

The pieces were all in place for Noelle now. "You killed the other girls because they looked like her." *I looked like her.* "You thought we'd give you the same rush, but we weren't Emma Jane, so you needed to try something else." Duncan had entered the man's life at the perfect time.

Or the worst.

"I was good at killing." Patrick's words were hard, biting and eerily reminiscent of what Thomas had once told her. Almost helplessly, Noelle's gaze slid to Thomas. He was glaring at the man behind bars. "Duncan made it worth my while. Duncan paid me for my work, and I had one hell of a time." His voice was calmer now. "After all, I'd lost my pickup man." His blue stare locked on Thomas. "Courtesy of the Dragon. And, damn, but Justin was good at picking the girls. The kid always knew exactly what I liked back then."

"We're going to need a list of all your victims." Families deserved to get closure. This man before her, he could've killed so many people.

But Patrick just smirked. "Like I'm the only killer in the room." He nodded toward Thomas. "Why don't we do some sharing? Get him to tell you all about his kills, and then I'll tell you mine."

She kept her shoulders locked. "I don't need to know about what Thomas did in battle—"

Patrick's laughter cut her off. "I'm not talking about battle. I'm talking about what he did…for fun. Like when he was down in Alabama. How many did you kill then? Not counting my pickup man, of course. Because he was probably just a bonus for you."

Thomas was as still as stone.

"Not gonna tell her? How about I start… It was a whole gang that went down, after you turned on them…."

His mission. Patrick couldn't learn about the EOD or about what covers Thomas had used over the years. "In a few hours, you're going to be transferred to a maximum-security holding facility. You won't get out again, and you'll be very, very lucky to see the light of day ever again."

But Patrick was still focused on Thomas. "When I first saw you with her, I didn't get a good look at you. You're good at changing your appearance, though, aren't you? Blending in. Showing people what you want 'em to see."

"If you cooperate, we can help you." Noelle doubted that there was actually much help Mercer would allow. Maybe a slightly bigger cell? No, probably not. This guy would be locked away forever. But what he didn't know...

"You're missing what's right in front of you!" Patrick exploded.

Noelle didn't flinch.

"He's a killer! Worse than me! You think he's some kind of hero? Don't you know what he did to you when he had you in that cabin?"

Goose bumps rose on Noelle's flesh.

This was the monster who'd tried to destroy her life.

"He's just like me," Patrick told her, and he was so smug. "Only...I bet he's killed *more* men than I have. Think about that the next time you decide to have sex with him in front of a fire."

He *had* been there.

Revulsion twisted her stomach.

Patrick was laughing again and— Thomas moved in a flash. His hand flew through the gap between the bars. He grabbed Patrick around the neck and yanked the man forward. Patrick's head slammed into the bars. Bones crunched, and Noelle was pretty sure the perp's nose broke. Judging by that spray of blood... Oh, yes, it was definitely a break.

Patrick started howling and swearing.

Thomas withdrew his hand, stepped back. His eyes were on Noelle. "He won't tell us anything. Leave him here. The boss can work him over later."

She was sure the interrogations the EOD conducted were probably very different from standard FBI techniques.

Her gaze slid to the cell. Patrick Porter could answer all of the questions that she had about her past. He could tell Noelle why he'd picked her. Why he'd picked them all.

But…

It won't happen.

The man enjoyed his power too much, and if they were going to break through to him, they had to take the power away. The best way to do that was to act as if he didn't matter.

"We're done." Noelle turned away from the killer. Talking to him made her skin crawl. She was sick of maintaining an icy image when, in truth, just being close to Patrick made her feel as if she were splintering apart on the inside.

"Done?" Patrick snarled. "We're done when I say! Now get me a doctor! He broke my damn nose!"

"Your nose is the least of your worries." Thomas sounded totally unconcerned. "Just wait until you get in your new home. That's when the real fun will begin."

Noelle grabbed for the door.

"Wait!" Patrick yelled after her. "You can't just leave me in here! I thought you wanted to deal! You wanted—"

Noelle glanced back at him. *Play the part. Play the part.* "Right now, I just want you to rot. You see, I think I was wrong. You don't have any information that I need to hear."

His face went slack with shock. Ah, nice. A new emotion.

She turned away from him and marched out of the holding area and didn't start shaking, not until the door closed behind Thomas. Not until they were away from the monster who'd changed her life.

Then her body trembled so hard she thought she'd collapse.

"Are you okay, Agent Evers?"

Her head jerked up at Aaron's question. He was a few feet away, frowning at her.

She didn't want him to see her break. All of the other EOD agents seemed to be so contained and strong. She couldn't crumble in front of him.

Thomas stepped in front of her, blocking Aaron's view. "She's fine. We're both exhausted, and we're getting some sleep before the plane takes off in a few hours." He jerked his thumb toward the closed door. "Keep a close eye on him. I don't trust the guy not to make some kind of last-ditch escape effort. Guys like him would rather go out with a bang than be chained up."

Then Thomas looked back at her. "She's fine," he said again, as he stared into Noelle's eyes.

Then he was pulling her down the narrow hallway. He shoved open the door to the office they'd commandeered before, and he hurried her inside.

When the door shut behind them, when they were finally alone, Noelle let the tears come.

Chapter Ten

It was a good thing bars had separated him from Patrick Porter because Thomas had sure wanted to do more than just break the man's nose.

That SOB had planned Noelle's murder. He'd been the one who intended to hunt her like an animal, then leave her remains in the woods of Alabama.

He'd been laughing, so smug and confidant.

And Noelle was crying.

Thomas stared at her a moment, and he felt absolutely lost. Her tears… They *hurt* him and seemed to strike out right at his heart. And she was hunching her shoulders and trying to cover her face so he wouldn't see. As if she needed to hide from him.

There was no part of Noelle that ever needed to be hidden from his sight. To him, every single inch of her was perfect.

He caught her hands, pulled them down and

held them tightly in his. Then Thomas bent toward her and pressed a kiss to her cheek. He could taste the salt of her tears. He *hated* her pain.

I want that man in the ground.

"What can I do?" Thomas knew the words sounded like little more than a growl, but his rage was too strong for anything else. "Tell me how to help you."

She shook her head and tried to pull away.

He just held her tighter, and he kissed her other cheek. Crying had always made him uncomfortable. Truth be told, emotion made him uncomfortable, but with Noelle, everything was different. Her hurt seemed to be his. He felt it slicing through him like a knife.

"I've seen men like him before." Her voice was soft. Husky with pain. "I've brought them in for the FBI. I've seen the broken victims left in their wake." She swallowed and whispered, "Now I'm one of them."

"No." A sharp comeback. "There is nothing broken about you. You're the strongest woman I've ever met."

She blinked up at him. Her eyes were so gorgeous, even glistening with tears. Hell, maybe they were more gorgeous that way. Did she have any clue she was bringing him to his knees? "You got away," he told her, fighting to keep his hold light on her. "You got away, and *you* were the one who finally brought down this jerk."

"The EOD—"

"We couldn't have done this without you, and you know it. It's not about being a victim. It's about being a survivor. Survivors are the brave ones. The powerful ones. That's you, baby. Through and through." He had to kiss her, so he did. Thomas lowered his head, and his lips brushed against hers. He'd meant for the kiss to be easy. Light.

At first, it was.

Her hands rose and curled around his shoulders. She pulled him closer and kissed him harder.

And the desire he felt for her raged hotter.

In an instant, the kiss wasn't about comforting her. It wasn't about taking away her pain. It was just about them. The consuming need they felt for each other.

He locked her against his body, holding her flush against him. She had to feel his desire, because there was certainly no hiding it.

Then she—

Pulled away.

Thomas sucked in a hard breath and clenched his hands into fists. Noelle didn't look at him as she backed off, putting a careful distance between them.

"Noelle..."

She jerked at his voice.

He frowned at her, then he remembered all of the things Patrick had said. Things he'd feared the man would say. Because he and Patrick Porter... Their paths had crossed before. Only back then, the man had been using an alias.

So had Thomas.

"It's not true," he told her. He needed her to look at him. Hell, he needed her back in his arms.

"I don't want to be here," Noelle said, her voice still whisper soft. She stalked for the door. Before she could leave, his hand flew out, and he shoved the wooden door closed.

"It's not true," he said once more.

Her head turned. Her eyes met his. She wasn't crying anymore, but there were secrets in her gaze. Thomas was pretty sure he'd sell his soul if it meant he could learn what they were.

"I didn't do anything to hurt you all those years ago, I swear." He had to make her believe that. It was so important she trust him.

Noelle blinked. Then she smiled. A slow smile that made him ache. Her hand rose and touched his cheek. "Oh, Thomas, I know that. You saved me then. I didn't doubt that truth for an instant."

For a moment, *he* was the one who couldn't speak. Her faith in him seemed so strong. Staggering. No one had ever believed in him the way she did. "I—" He broke off, cleared his throat and tried again. "I need you to know that I have met that man before."

He felt the tension that hardened her body. "When?"

Aw, damn, this was going to hurt the most. "When I was working undercover in Alabama." So long ago. "I got the intel I needed on that group, and the EOD stormed in, but before I did…I had to pass the group's initiation."

"What did you do?"

Her voice was so hoarse.

"I fought four men."

She pulled away from him.

"I didn't kill them, I swear, but…if I hadn't fought, they would've pegged me for an agent. I had to prove myself." He had. "There were three of us there for the initiation. A group circled us, threw back in the men who tried to run. Porter— I turned once and he was in front of me. He knew I wasn't one of the ones running. He was laughing." He swallowed bile. "Cheering me on as I attacked." *Dragon, Dragon!* He'd just gone by that tag back then, to better fit in with the group.

The guy had even come up and congratulated him on a good fight afterward.

She paled before him. "I have to get out of here. I just— I need to leave."

He was afraid she was leaving him. "I was undercover. My job was to infiltrate and bring down that organization."

"No matter the cost."

She'd been the cost.

Thomas shook his head. "If I'd known for a minute that he was the man who'd arranged your abduction—"

"Why didn't the EOD apprehend him then? If the rest of the group got *contained,* then why not him?" Emotion ripped through her words. Pain. Fury. "Why was he left free to hurt and kill?"

"Because he wasn't there when the EOD team came in. Something had spooked him and he ran."

Her laugh was cold. Mocking. "*I* spooked him."

Thomas frowned at her.

"He must've gone back to hunt me. I wasn't there, the cops were, so he knew he had to clear out." A bitter smile twisted her lips. "No one else had seen him there, so he just slipped away. Or, sailed away, I guess, since he just boarded the naval vessel and headed to the next port."

Then he'd kept killing. Only his prey had changed, and he'd started working with a new partner.

"I'm sorry," Thomas told her. The words weren't enough. They never would be. For so many years, he'd hated the choices he'd made. A young girl, left alone. He hadn't realized that someone else was out there, possibly still after her.

"So am I," Noelle said. Then she jerked open the door and straightened her shoulders. When she left this time, he didn't follow her. He knew she wanted to get away.

From me.

So he let her go.

"THIS ISN'T OVER!" Patrick Porter yelled as he grabbed the bars. The woman had left and the agent—*Dragon, you liar*—had followed on her heels.

They thought they were done? That they just got to walk away while he was tossed into a cell to rot?

No. That wasn't the way his story would be ending.

"The blood's gonna be on you!" His bellow seemed to echo back to him. "Another body... *on you, Noelle!* You thought it was bad when you were the victim? How's it gonna feel when you realize you let her die? *You. Let. Her. Die!*"

AARON BLACK FROWNED as he glanced toward the holding-room door. The jerk in there had been yelling his head off for the past ten minutes. Making threats. Demanding his freedom.

Talking about a victim.

It could be pure bull, of course. A last-ditch effort to save himself. Aaron had seen it before. When facing nothing but a dark cell for endless days, men would lie. They'd promise anything. Everything. Tell any falsehood imaginable.

But…

Sometimes, they would also tell the truth.

He stepped closer to the holding room.

NOELLE STOOD IN the snow. Her eyes were closed. Her hands outstretched. She was just a few feet away from the sheriff's station. A monster was inside that station. A man with a soul darker than hell.

She had to face him again. It was her job. But every time she looked into his eyes, Noelle felt as if she were a helpless teen again. Lost and so scared.

Waiting to die.

Snow crunched to the left, and in an instant, Noelle spun around with her gun up.

Her firearm locked right on Bruce Mercer. He lifted his hands toward her. "Easy. I'm not the enemy."

Sometimes, it was hard to tell which side Mercer was really on. "You kept my past from me." She holstered her weapon.

"I thought the danger was gone." He exhaled and advanced toward her. "I was very wrong."

Her eyebrows shot up. Had the great and oh, so powerful Mercer just admitted to being wrong? Human?

"You weren't alone."

She had no idea what he was talking about.

"Has Agent Anthony told you that part yet?"

"He told me that he'd seen Porter. While he was undercover in Alabama, Thomas *saw* him with that terrorist group."

"Ah, yes, well, is it surprising that Porter would have ties to others who wanted to maim and kill? Like to like, you know."

Yes, she knew plenty about the darkness that hid within men.

"We didn't have an ID on Porter then. Just a basic physical description. He slipped away." Mercer heaved out a breath as he stared at the mountains in the distance. "We try our hardest, but there are always some that get away. For every killer we stop, another one is out there, waiting in the wings." His voice lowered. "Some days I wonder if it will ever end."

She rubbed her arms. The snow had felt good before, seeming to cool the fire that burned within her as it fell again, but now…

"Thomas was at the hospital because he needed to see you. He even went in your room, but you didn't recognize him. You didn't know him at all."

Those words had her breath catching.

"Maybe Thomas told you he'd watched you over the years, but I don't think you realize… quite how much. When your mother died, he was at the funeral. When your father passed, he was at the nursing home. When you graduated from college, he was in the audience. When you went on your first case with the FBI, he was shadowing you."

She could only shake her head. That made no sense to her. *"Why?"*

"Because fifteen years ago, Thomas Anthony met a girl in the woods. A girl he said was the bravest, strongest person he'd ever met. He told me the girl was hurt and scared, but she kept fighting to survive, no matter what."

She looked away from Mercer. She didn't want him reading the expression in her eyes.

"Because fifteen years ago…" Mercer said again. "I think a twenty-two-year-old agent fell in love with that girl. With her strength and her courage, and he couldn't bear to imagine her alone in the world. He wanted to keep her safe. To watch over her. So he did, in his way, and with every year that passed, every day that he watched her prove again and again just how strong she was, I think he fell for her even more."

No, no, that couldn't be true. "He would've said something to me."

Mercer laughed at that.

Her head whipped back around toward him. She could *never* remember hearing Mercer laugh.

"Thomas Anthony is a good agent. One of the best I've ever seen, but that man doesn't connect easily with others. He keeps his emotions to himself."

"Then how do you know—"

"Because you're not the only one who is good at reading people. And if you weren't so blinded by your own feelings, you'd see that Thomas Anthony would die in an instant, if it meant keeping you safe. He'd lie, he'd kill, he'd cheat. He'd do anything for you."

Her heart was thundering in her chest. "Why are you telling me this?" *Now?*

"Because the mission ends in just a few

hours. When we board the plane, that's the end for your partnership with Thomas Anthony."

Noelle shook her head. "But the EOD—"

"Oh, don't worry about us. We'll always be around." He gave a little nod. "But your period as an EOD liaison from the FBI, that's over."

It was the last thing she'd expected. "You're *firing* me?"

His lips twitched. "No. I brought you on because I thought being around Anthony would stir some memories, and if that didn't work, I thought, well…" His words trailed away. But surely, Bruce Mercer wasn't suggesting he'd tried to play matchmaker for her and Thomas? Mercer was a power player. Not some closet romantic who—

"You deserve some happiness. So does he." Mercer rubbed his chin. "I'm not saying I won't be using you again. You're the best profiler I've ever come across, but in the future, you won't be partnered with Anthony. So whatever you two decide, there's nothing at the EOD that will stand between you." His hand dropped as he gazed at her. "The only thing between the two of you is what you put there. Ghosts from your past. Fears about your future. It's all what *you* see…or what you don't."

He pointed down the road. "Thomas went back to the cabin you two rented. He said he was tired. Maybe you should go there and try to get a little shut-eye, too." Then he turned and made his way back inside the sheriff's station.

Noelle sucked in a deep gulp of air. One. Two.

Then she found herself hurrying forward. She got the keys to the extra rental truck, and she was on her way back to the cabin before she gave herself a second to think.

She parked the truck and hurried inside the cabin. She opened her mouth to call out to Thomas, but stopped when she caught sight of him near the fireplace.

He wore only a pair of loose jogging pants. His back was to her. Strong, broad. He was moving fluidly, as his hands struck out above him and his feet lifted in a series of blurring kicks.

Martial arts. She didn't recognize any of his moves but she'd read in his file he'd studied tae kwon do, jujitsu, krav maga and aikido.

She shut the door behind her then leaned back against the wall and just watched him.

Admired him.

His muscles stretched. Flexed. His skin gleamed golden in the firelight. He turned to the left. Then the right. His strikes were fast and powerful.

And she kept watching.

Noelle wasn't sure how much time passed, but after a while, Thomas turned to slowly face her. His eyes seemed to reflect the fire.

"What was…?" She stopped, cleared her throat and tried again. "What was that?"

"Choong-Jang, a black belt form for tae kwon do." He rolled back his shoulders and regarded her with a locked jaw.

"Does that…help you relax?"

"Sometimes." He shook his head and took a step toward her. "Not this time."

She tensed. Mercer's words seemed to echo through her mind. She wanted to ask Thomas if the EOD director's story was true. Had Thomas really been there, in the background for so much of her life?

She stopped less than a foot away from him. Helplessly, her gaze slid over his body. The man had a truly magnificent chest. So muscled. Strong.

"The scars will always be there."

Her gaze jerked up to his face. "I wasn't looking at your scars." She'd been more focused on the muscles.

His laughter was rough. "They slide all across me. It's hard to miss them."

"I think I was distracted by other things," she murmured, aware her cheeks were stinging.

One dark brow rose.

She tried to pull in a steadying breath. It didn't work so much. Noelle didn't feel steady at all. She was nervous. Tense. And...

"We go back to D.C. soon," she blurted.

He nodded.

"Mercer told me that my job as an FBI liaison with the EOD is done. For now, anyway."

That news had him frowning. "You're leaving?"

I don't want to leave him.

"How often have you watched me?" The question slipped from her.

His hand rose to stroke her cheek. "I don't want to scare you. I *never* want to do that."

She turned her head and kissed his palm. She felt the tension thicken around them. "You don't." The darkness that clung to him had never frightened her. The power he possessed just made her feel safe because Noelle knew he'd protect her.

It was what he'd always done.

"I used to dream about you," he whispered, the words rough. "At first, the dreams were the girl I left in that cabin. You were scared and you were crying out for me."

Pain echoed in his voice.

"I'm not scared any longer." She'd worked hard to become stronger.

"Then the dreams changed because *you*

changed." His hand slid away from her as his shoulders straightened. "I started to dream about the woman you'd become."

Maybe…maybe Mercer was right. "What do you want from me?" Noelle asked him and she held her breath as she waited for his response.

At his sides, Thomas's hands balled into fists. "I'm a desperate man. I've been that way…too long." His gaze held hers. "I want whatever you'll give me."

I'll give you everything. Maybe she already had. She moved toward him and eliminated that little bit of space. Her hands curled around his shoulders. Then Noelle put her lips on his.

She was making a choice. Choosing *him.* Noelle needed Thomas to understand that. Just as she needed him to choose her. Her mouth moved lightly on his, caressing.

His hands rose and locked around her hips. She could feel the strength of his arousal pressing against her.

"I don't want just one more night." His words were growled against her lips. "With you, I want forever. I can't have another taste just to lose you when we leave this place."

His words broke her heart. Noelle shook her head. "You won't lose me." He was what she wanted. The past was done. The ghosts—

dead. She wanted to focus on the future, and she wasn't going to let any fears hold her back.

Mercer had been right on that score.

Thomas kissed her again, and the kiss was harder. Deeper. He took control, and she felt the passion pour through her. She couldn't get close enough to him. Couldn't feel him enough.

They stumbled together up the stairs. When she slipped, his grasp on her tightened. He lifted her up, holding her easily.

She kept kissing him.

Then they were in the bedroom. He tugged off her clothes, stripping her quickly, and her hands swept over his shoulders. His chest.

He eased her toward the bed, but Noelle didn't fall back on the mattress. Instead, she lowered to her knees before him, and her lips skimmed over the scars on his chest and stomach. Scars that mattered to him but not to her. The scars told her how strong he was. How he'd survived.

But that was all.

To her, Thomas was perfect.

He caught her hands, though, when her lips skimmed low on his stomach, and he pushed her back. "I can't—" His words ended in a growl as he lifted her up and settled her on the bed.

This wasn't about seduction or finesse. This

was about need and desire in its most primal, pure form.

He ditched the rest of his clothes. His fingers caught hers, pinned them to the bed. With his eyes on her, he thrust inside. Her breath caught as he surged deep, then her legs lifted and wrapped around him. She held him tight, and when he began to thrust, she met him, arching her body eagerly.

They rolled over the bed, twisting and turning as the passion surged hotter and harder. Her nails scraped over his back. The pleasure was just out of her reach. *So close.*

His fingers freed hers. He touched her between her legs, finding just the spot that had her gasping, then shuddering in release.

He was with her. Thrusting deep and hard. Shaking the bed. Shaking her. Making the pleasure ripple through her once more.

"Too…good…" He groaned the words. "Can't…get enough…with you…."

Noelle felt the same way with him. She wondered if it would ever be enough, or if the need would grow and—

He drove into her once more.

Pleasure lashed through her.

His release swept over him, stiffening Thomas's body, and he held her in a grip of steel.

Noelle couldn't catch her breath. Her heart

raced frantically, the sound a drumbeat in her ears. She was panting hard, her whole body quaking, and she tried to grab back control because there was something very important she needed to tell him.

I love you.

The truth had hit her when she was at the sheriff's station. When Porter had tried to shatter her trust in Thomas, and she'd realized *nothing* could break her trust in him.

Not because he was her partner.

But because he was the man who'd worked his way into her heart.

Her lips parted.

Thomas kissed her again.

"YOU'RE KILLING HER!" Patrick yelled, his voice echoing back to him. "This one won't be on me! It's on you! *All of you!*"

The holding room door flew open and banged against the wall.

Patrick lowered his head so the man who'd rushed in wouldn't see his smile.

"You had your chance to talk," the guy snarled. "You didn't. If you can't stop the screams, then I'll just shove a gag in your mouth."

Patrick's head snapped up. "That's not the way cops work."

"Who said I was a cop?" The man demanded.

Thomas stared into the fellow's cold eyes. He took in the guy's battle-ready posture. The hands, which were loose at his sides and the grim face, which could've been staring into hell.

I'll show him hell.

"You'll be leaving this place in about three hours," the man told him flatly. "Settle down until then, or I will settle you down."

Patrick stared back at him. Didn't speak.

The guy gave a grim nod and turned away. Patrick waited until the fellow reached for the door.

"She'll still be alive in three hours," Patrick mused. "At least, I think she will. Guess it depends on how long she can stand the cold out there, all alone."

The man glanced back at him. Patrick knew the guy was trying to judge him. To see if he was telling the truth or if he was just spinning a new lie.

"I got tired of Lawrence Duncan sending me out to do *his* work. I was tired of killing for him," he waited a beat, then added slyly, "and for her."

"Her?" The guy's brows climbed.

Patrick gave a slow nod. "They were working together. Always were. She would slip in and get the intel he needed. People talk so much easier to a pretty face, and Paula sure has a pretty face." He whistled, remembering the other features he enjoyed about her. "But I figured, if I'm done with Duncan, then I'm done with her, too."

"You're trying to say you've abducted—"

"The senator's aide, Paula Quill." His fingers curled around the bars. "And if you want her to keep living, *you'll get me out of here!*"

Chapter Eleven

He wasn't going to let her go. Thomas lifted his head and stared down into Noelle's unforgettable eyes as he tried to find the right words to tell her. No one had ever meant as much to him as she did, and the last thing he wanted to do was mess up anything with her.

He'd already botched things enough already. He had to use care.

And not bulldoze his way ahead.

He withdrew from her body, hating the separation because the woman felt like heaven. If he had his way, he'd stay curled with her for hours. Days.

But…

Duty waited.

So did the plane.

Before they boarded and left Alaska, he needed to clear the air between them.

But his phone was ringing. Thomas frowned as the buzzing reached him. The sound was coming from downstairs because he'd left it down there earlier. When Noelle had kissed him, answering it had been the last thing on his mind.

Noelle blinked, obviously hearing the sound, too. "Ah, are you expecting someone?"

No, Mercer had said they were clear until takeoff. He brushed his hand over the silken length of her arm. "I'll be right back. Don't... don't move, okay? We need to talk." As soon as he could figure out how to say the right words.

She gave a slow nod.

Thomas yanked on his jogging pants and hurried downstairs. The caller wasn't giving up; that was for sure. Thomas grabbed the phone, then tensed when he saw the number on the screen. He lifted the phone to his ear. "Anthony."

"Do you know where Paula Quill is right now?" Aaron demanded.

Thomas glanced toward the stairs. "The senator's aide? She's been staying at his house in Camden, so check for her there."

"We did. We've called and sent a deputy over to that place, but the staff there say that they haven't seen her since before the big storm swept in."

"So she went out to visit friends before the bad weather hit." His eyes were still on the stairs. He didn't hear any sound from overhead. "Get the woman's cell number and—"

"We've called her cell." Tension deepened Aaron's voice. "There's no answer."

Thomas hesitated. "Why are her whereabouts so important to you?"

"Because that joker in lockup is screaming that he has her hidden in the wilderness, and he says the only way she makes it out alive is if he goes back in for her."

"What?"

"So we need you and Noelle back at the station, right now. Because if he's not lying…"

Thomas's gaze was now on the darkness beyond the window. *If Patrick is telling the truth, then Paula Quill could be out there right now, dying.*

Thomas ended the call and raced back up the stairs. As soon as Noelle saw his expression, she leapt to her feet. "What's happening?"

"Patrick Porter may have taken another victim." They wouldn't know for sure, not yet, but… "We have to get back to the station."

She yanked on her clothes. "Who's the victim?"

He dressed quickly, his movement jerky. "Paula Quill."

"The senator's aide?" She shook her head. "What do you think…? Is he—is he lying?"

Thomas hoped so, but a knot had formed in his gut. They finished dressing. When she started to rush past him, Thomas caught her arm. "Before we go, there's something I need you to know." Because he never wanted secrets between them again.

Noelle glanced back at him.

I don't want to mess this up. She means too much to me. The woman deserved wining and dining, not some rushed confession on their way to interrogate a prisoner.

"Thomas? What is it?"

"I will not leave you again." The words rumbled, too deep. "You can count on me, no matter what."

Her smile came then, spreading slowly over her face and lighting her eyes. "I already knew that."

Okay. *Do it.* "Did you know I love you?"

Wait. Hell, he'd meant that to come out better. But charm had never been his strong suit.

She blinked up at him.

He cleared his throat. "I wanted you to know that." He knew she didn't love him, but maybe they could have *something* when they went back to D.C. "I don't want us to end when the plane touches back down in D.C."

"Thomas—"

"Let's finish this case. Find out if Porter is

telling the truth or just jerking us around and then…" He pushed back his shoulders. "Give me the chance to prove that you and I can work out. We can have something together." *Something worth fighting for.*

Her gaze searched his. Thomas wasn't sure what she was looking for. If he knew, he'd give her everything she needed. "Noelle—"

His phone started ringing again.

Damn it!

"Give me the chance," Thomas said again. Then there was nothing more to say. They had a killer to face.

"WE FOUND THESE images on Patrick Porter's phone." Mercer's voice was grim.

Noelle stared down at the images. They showed a familiar woman—Paula Quill—tied to a chair. A blindfold covered her eyes.

"The jerk *told* us where to find the images on his phone. He's taunting us, and he likes the power he has," Mercer added.

Noelle looked up at the EOD boss.

"No one has seen Paula Quill in over twenty-four hours," Mercer said.

"No one but Patrick," Thomas said. "The time stamp on that image is six hours ago."

Six hours. Time to live. Time to die.

Her gaze slid toward the holding-room door.

"He told Aaron that he'd lead us to Paula." Mercer paused. "No, he said he'd lead *you* to her, Agent Evers."

"That's not happening!" Thomas snapped. "No way is Noelle going out in the wilderness with that guy!"

"Yes, well, I figured you'd say that, Anthony." Mercer started to pace. "If the woman is out there, we need the search dogs. We need to patrol the area and find—"

"The area is too big. He left her out there to die." Noelle's voice was certain. She turned back to face Mercer. "He knew we were closing in. He wanted leverage." No wonder he'd been so willing to sacrifice the other women. He'd had a backup plan all along. His ace in case he was captured. "Paula Quill is that leverage. If we don't agree to go after her, then Paula is dead."

Mercer shook his head. "The EOD—"

Noelle's hand lifted. "Doesn't negotiate. Right. I've heard the spiel before." She pulled in a deep breath. "But I'm not EOD, not any longer. I got fired, remember? Now I'm back to being plain old FBI."

Mercer studied her, his eyes narrowed.

"I'm not letting a woman die on my watch."

Thomas surged toward her. "He sets traps.

You know his game. And you're just going to walk out with him—"

She laughed. "No, *we* are." Because if Patrick had said he'd only take her to find Paula, then she knew exactly what he intended to do. "Patrick Porter wants me dead. I was the first victim who got away. He wants me out there, where he's in control. He wants to kill me because I'm the one who came back and destroyed everything for him."

A muscle flexed in Thomas's jaw. "I'm *not* letting that happen."

Right. She nodded. "I knew I could count on you."

His brows shot up.

"You come with us. You watch my back. I'll watch yours. We'll get Paula out—"

"How do you know the guy will even lead you to her?" Mercer demanded as his words cut through hers.

Noelle had to shrug. "He wants me to see what he can do. It's all a game to him."

But he wasn't going to win the game. She was. No matter what she had to do, she'd beat him.

She headed toward the holding room. Mercer caught her arm. "He said that Paula Quill was working with the senator. That she helped gather intel and plan hits on the senator's targets."

Her eyes widened. *Paula isn't just an innocent victim.* "And you think she was tied to the attack on the EOD."

"She's a person of interest." His lips tightened into a thin line. "I need her brought in alive."

Because Mercer still wanted to know why the EOD had been set up for the attack in the first place.

"You've both got current tracking devices?" Mercer asked, frowning at them.

At the EOD, all agents had small devices implanted just beneath the skin. If his agents were taken by the enemy, Mercer wanted to be able to make certain they were rescued, no matter where they went.

Thomas nodded. So did Noelle. She'd gotten her chip right after she'd started in her liaison role.

Mercer's attention shifted to Thomas. "Never let her out of your sight."

"Don't worry—it won't happen." Thomas was adamant.

Mercer held his stare a little longer, then he stepped back. He waved toward the holding-room door. "Do what you need to do."

Noelle straightened her shoulders and marched forward. She schooled her expression so no emotion showed on her face when she entered the holding room—and saw Patrick in his cell. He smirked at her. He was so confident of his control and power. She needed to destroy that confidence. She *would*.

Aaron stood just a few feet away, and he was glaring at their prisoner.

"Saw my pictures, did you?" Patrick asked her, voice nearly purring with satisfaction. "I was wondering how long it would take you to see them."

"Why didn't you tell us—immediately—that you'd taken her?" Noelle asked.

"I *would've* told you, but you're the one who stopped talking to me." His eyes sparked with fury. "So if she dies, you're the one to blame for that."

Thomas stalked to Noelle's side. "You really think you're just going to walk out of here with Agent Evers?"

"I think if I don't go, you'll never find Paula."

His voice had softened a bit when he said the other woman's name. Because she was his victim and he enjoyed his victims so much?

Enjoyed their suffering, their pain.

Noelle's head inclined a bit as she studied him.

"Paula will vanish and her death will be on you two." He shook his head. "And here I thought you were supposed to save people."

"We did save Jenny," Noelle pointed out to him because she wanted to see his response.

The fury flashed in his eyes again. *"Jenny,"* he bit out the name, "wasn't worth my time. She wasn't a challenge. She wasn't anything to me. Just bait, to lure you out."

"Isn't that what Paula is, too?" Thomas wanted to know. "Bait. You stick her in the middle of nowhere, and you expect us to just follow your lead...right into whatever hell you've got waiting for us?"

Patrick laughed. "You have to do it! Because if you don't, you both know she's dead." He pointed toward Noelle. *"She* can't live with a death on her. You..." He waved dismissively toward Thomas. "You don't care. People don't matter to you."

Yes, they did. He didn't know Thomas at all.

Patrick's eyes were on Noelle. "But she won't let an innocent die. She can't. Seeing Paula tied up like that, it was like seeing yourself, wasn't it?"

She didn't let any emotion break through. "You're a control freak, a man who thinks that he's the strongest and the toughest in any room that he enters. But you weren't always that way. In fact, you first killed Emma Jane because you felt weak." She was about to show him just how much she knew. "You got a rush from her death, one unlike anything you'd ever felt before."

He was still smirking at her. *That smirk is going to vanish.*

"I don't think you meant to *hunt* her. I think Emma Jane got away from you. She ran. You had to chase her. That's when you began to like the hunt so much."

His smirk slipped.

"You tried to recreate that rush by taking girls who reminded you of Emma Jane, but that just didn't work." She shook her head. "Then, of course, you found out your partner had been killed. That made you feel lost, isolated—and powerless. You hate to feel like you lack power—"

"Because I don't! I never lack power!"

"Lucky for you, though, Duncan entered the picture then. He used you, but he also refocused you. The rush came back because your prey was more challenging, and you continued this way…for a while."

His breath heaved out. "You think you're so smart—"

"It was only a matter of time until you killed him. You couldn't keep following his orders forever, even if you enjoyed the work. Following *his* orders meant he held power, not you. So when he pushed too far, when he told you to kill me and Agent Anthony *his* way, you snapped."

Patrick glared at her. *And the smirk is gone.*

"You'll always snap in the end." Noelle sighed as if she pitied him. She didn't. She hated him. "Control is your weakness."

His hands flew out from behind the bars, lunging toward her, but he was too far away to do any damage. His fingers stretched uselessly into the air.

"You think you'll get power by taking me into the wilderness, leading me on a hunt for Paula, then killing me." She glanced from his hands to his face. "That won't happen."

"Your death is overdue," he snarled at her.

"So is yours," Thomas fired right back.

Patrick's hands jerked backed through the bars.

"I go with you," Thomas said, voice hard. "You're cuffed, and you're within sight at all times. You take us to Paula and—"

"And what do I get?"

Noelle knew it wasn't really about what he'd get. Obviously, the man planned to try and kill them out there. But she played along, for now. "You get to walk outside once a day when you get to your future prison home. You can see the sun, and not live every single minute pinned behind bars."

She waited.

Patrick's jaw was clenched.

"Deal?" Noelle pressed because she didn't know how much time Paula had left.

"Deal," Patrick snarled. But his eyes… His eyes were glinting with triumph.

THOMAS STAYED RIGHT beside Noelle as they approached the cabin. A helicopter had brought them in as they'd followed Patrick Porter's gritted instructions.

Those instructions had taken them back to the general area where they'd found Sarah Finway's body. Where Patrick had been waiting to attack them all before.

Had Sarah seen Paula? Had the two women been kept together? And when Patrick decided he needed to make one of them scream, had Sarah been his unlucky choice?

Noelle had seen Thomas's face tense as they drew closer to the area, and she knew the same questions were plaguing him. Had they been so close to another victim and hadn't even realized it?

The chopper had landed and it waited a good two hundred yards away. They'd trudged through the snow and the woods. Patrick was cuffed and far too confident.

That confidence was about to end.

It wasn't the first time a prisoner had offered an exchange to Noelle. It also wasn't the first time Noelle knew that prisoner was planning a double cross.

A death.

Aaron was shadowing them. He'd been the one flying the chopper, and Noelle knew the guy hadn't stayed behind. He was just remaining out of Patrick's sight as he trailed them, waiting for the moment to strike.

They cleared a deep thatch of trees, and Noelle saw the cabin. It was nestled under the broader trees, its exterior nearly covered by thick snow. No wonder they hadn't spotted it from the sky. It was too well camouflaged.

"Built it myself," Patrick said as he expelled a rush of air, which appeared as a white cloud before his face. "That way, I knew no one would ever be able to find the place." He waved his hand. "Go on in… She's waiting for you."

Right. As if they were idiots.

Thomas lifted his weapon and pointed at Patrick. "You could have the place rigged to blow. As soon as we walk in, boom."

Patrick just shrugged. "I could…"

Noelle's gaze returned to the cabin. Something about this scene nagged at her.

Snow crunched beneath Thomas's boots. "And that's why you're going in first."

Patrick opened his mouth to reply.

"There's no smoke," Noelle said. She glanced around.

"'Course, there's no smoke," Patrick muttered. "She's tied up. She can't start a fire, and I sure as hell wasn't starting one. Why give away the place's position?"

No fire…but also no pile of snow in front of the door. It had been snowing off and on during the past seven hours. It was particularly heavy right after they brought Patrick into the sheriff's station. If no one had been at that cabin in hours, the snow should've piled up in front of the door. Instead, it looked as if the path to the door had been freshly cleared.

Something glinted in the window of the little cabin.

Her eyes widened as Noelle realized she was staring at the barrel of a gun. She started to scream a warning to Thomas, but he was already moving. He grabbed her, wrapping his arms around her, and she slammed back into the ground just as the thunder of gunfire exploded.

Gunfire…and laughter. Patrick's laughter.

She spat snow out of her mouth and tried to shove up, but Thomas wasn't letting her go.

"Shooter in the cabin," he growled into her ear.

Because Patrick *had* found another partner.

"Can't see him," Thomas whispered. "But he has eyes on us."

Patrick was running toward the cabin.

"Stop!" Thomas yelled at the guy.

Patrick only ran faster. Another shot blasted from the cabin.

And a shot also blasted from Thomas's gun. The bullet caught Patrick in the shoulder. The man spun around, snarling.

Thunder echoed once more. No, not thunder. The roar was more gunfire, coming from the cabin. The bullet ripped right past Noelle's head, so close she felt its heat against her.

"We need cover," Thomas said, "*Now.* You run for the thicker trees, and I'll watch your back."

Translation—she ran and he fired, making himself a target. Not a plan she loved. Not even one she liked. Noelle yanked out her own weapon.

Patrick was stumbling toward that cabin door. He was close, just about five feet away from the entrance.

Gunfire erupted once more. Patrick's body jerked when he was hit, his body moving like a marionette on a string. Blood sprayed into the snow, turning it red.

Patrick's partner had just shot him. Noelle

sure hadn't seen that coming. Noelle had thought she and Thomas were the targets.

"Go!" Thomas yelled to Noelle.

Patrick slipped. Fell.

Thomas fired into the cabin. Noelle rushed to the cover of the woods, and Thomas was right behind her.

And—and Aaron was there. She saw the darkness of his hair, and he started shooting, providing cover fire for her and Thomas as they got to safety.

When Noelle turned back again, Patrick was lying in the snow, and the red beneath him was spreading.

"What in the hell is happening?" Aaron demanded. "I thought this was a rescue mission!'

Thomas shook his head and never took his gaze from the cabin. "It was a trap, all along."

"For us? Or for that jerk out there, bleeding out?"

Patrick was moaning and begging for help.

Fury and fear churned within Noelle. *Did your victims beg, too?*

"Is the woman in there?" Aaron wanted to know.

They hadn't gotten a glimpse of the shooter, not yet.

But Noelle didn't need a glimpse. "She is."

Aaron grunted. "So, we're looking at two people in—"

"Only one," Noelle interrupted. "Just one."

As comprehension sank in, Aaron whistled. "Paula Quill got free and found a gun in the place, huh? Payback is a—"

The cabin's door opened then. A small, hunched figure appeared.

Paula.

She had a gun in her hand. She lifted the gun and aimed it at the begging Patrick.

Paula walked forward. Her grip on the gun was steady and her steps were slow.

She's going to kill him.

"Stop!" Thomas shouted.

Paula's head jerked up. So did her gun. She pointed it at Thomas.

"No, Thomas," Noelle said as Thomas stepped forward, "that woman isn't a victim." Noelle was seeing her for exactly what she was.

Patrick's partner.

Paula fired. So did Thomas. His bullet hit its target, and Paula fell back, slamming into the side of the cabin.

But her bullet had hit, too. Thomas's blood sprayed in the air, and Noelle gave a frantic cry as she grabbed for him.

No, not Thomas. Not—

Aaron sprang forward, running toward Paula.

Thomas grabbed Noelle's hand. Blood streamed from a wound near his upper arm. "Just a flesh wound, baby. I swear, I'm fine."

And she realized she'd been pleading, so desperate for him to be all right.

His hold tightened on her. "It would take a lot more than this to slow me down."

Yes, yes, it would. Relief had her feeling light-headed, but they didn't have time to waste. She and Thomas rushed after Aaron.

The other agent had already kicked the gun away from Paula. Paula's wound was almost an exact mirror image of Thomas's.

But Paula was screaming, and Thomas was eerily silent.

Aaron locked his hand around Paula's uninjured shoulder. "Wrong move, ma'am, *wrong*."

"Help...me..." Patrick pleaded when Noelle drew closer to him.

She stared down at his bloody chest. His breath was wheezing in and out. If he didn't get medical attention, he'd be dead in moments.

Noelle dropped to her knees beside him.

"What are you doing?" Paula shrieked. "Let him die! After what he did to you, *let him bleed out!*"

Noelle shook her head. "That's not who I am." She ripped his shirt away. Saw the gaping wounds. She tried to apply pressure.

"He has to die!" Paula screamed. "He killed Lawrence! He abducted me! *Let. Him. Die!"* She started sobbing then, deep, wrenching sobs, which shook her whole body.

Aaron swore. "Look, it's going to be all right…"

Noelle frantically shook her head. "He didn't abduct her—"

But it was too late. Aaron had lowered his guard, and Paula—Paula grabbed his gun.

She lifted the weapon, aimed for her target. But her target was right behind Noelle, and when Paula fired, standing less than five feet away while Noelle crouched on the cold snow, Noelle knew that bullet was going to hit her. It would hit her, then go *through* her as it rushed toward Patrick Porter.

She tried to brace herself. *Thomas, I—*

The bullet didn't hit her.

Thomas jumped in front of Noelle.

The bullet hit him, and Noelle screamed.

He had his gun up, but Thomas didn't get the chance to fire. The weapon slipped from his hands as he staggered back and fell into her. Noelle wrapped her arms around him. Held him tight. "Thomas, *Thomas!"*

Aaron wrestled the gun from Paula. The woman crumpled then, crying pitifully, but Noelle knew it was all an act. A show.

Thomas slumped against Noelle.

She felt the stickiness of his blood. Not from the wound near his shoulder, but from the wound at his heart.

He hit the snow beside her. She grabbed for him, shaking him. "Thomas!" His eyes were closed.

The wound... Desperately, quickly, Noelle looked for the entrance wound. An inch from his heart. But there was no exit wound. If there'd been an exit wound, she would've been hit, too. Instead, the bullet was lodged inside him.

Her head whipped toward Aaron. "We have to get him to the chopper, *now!*" Thomas's blood wasn't just on her fingers now. He was bleeding so much that the blood coated her hands.

No, no, no.

Aaron swore and rushed toward her, pulling Paula in his wake. The woman was still sobbing, still—

"I...love you..."

Thomas's rasped words had pain welling within Noelle. She held him tight, tried to stop that precious blood from pumping out of him. "I love you, too!"

His eyes were still closed and with every second that passed, he seemed to be growing paler.

"Thomas, I love you, too! Do you hear me?"

She didn't think he did.

Terror clawed through her.

"You said you wouldn't leave me alone. Not ever again."

He barely seemed to be breathing.

"Don't leave me. *Don't.*" She pressed a kiss to his lips. "I. Love. You."

But Thomas didn't answer her. When Mercer and two deputies rushed through the woods moments later, Thomas was unconscious. Unresponsive.

They loaded him into the helicopter. Patrick was pushed in beside him.

Patrick was still wheezing. His color had turned ashen. Thomas... She couldn't hear his breaths at all.

She held him tight. *I won't let you go.* "Keep your promise," she whispered as the tears burned her eyes. Then she looked toward the open door of the chopper.

Aaron stood there. A deputy had cuffed a sobbing Paula.

"Don't let her go!" Noelle cried out. "She's the key to this mess."

Paula's head lifted. Her gaze darted from Patrick to Thomas.

Paula smiled.

The chopper lifted in the air.

THOMAS KNEW HE was in a hospital even before he opened his eyes. It was the smell that told him, that antiseptic scent and the steady beeping of a nearby machine.

He remembered getting shot. Remembered the desperate fear he wouldn't get to Noelle in time to save her. So when he forced his eyes open and struggled to speak, her name was the first word he uttered. "No...elle..."

"I'm right here." Her hand squeezed his. "Do you hear me? I'm right here."

He turned his head. The glow of the sun was behind her, and damn if the woman didn't look like an angel to him.

His perfect dream. Right there.

"You're smiling." Noelle sounded worried. "Is that because of the drugs? Because when a person takes a bullet to the chest, a smile after surgery isn't the typical response."

Thomas shook his head.

"I'm calling the nurse." She lunged toward the call button.

"I...remember."

Noelle paused at his gruff words. "You remember the shooting? That's good. I was—I was worried you'd—"

He shook his head again, turning slightly against the pillow. Surprisingly, he felt no pain. Must've been the drugs. Like pain would've mattered to him right then. No, not when he *knew*. "You...love me."

He wondered if she would deny it.

"Of course, I love you," Noelle said as she bent close to him. Her beautiful eyes gleamed with tears. "I'm just surprised you didn't realize it sooner. I mean, I could barely get within ten feet of you without stumbling over my words every time we talked."

He'd thought that was fear. That he made her too nervous.

Noelle pressed a light kiss to his lips. "You're the most dangerous man I've ever met, and you're the only man who has ever made me feel completely safe when I'm with him."

His heart ached, and that wasn't due to the wound. "I'd die to keep you safe."

A tear spilled from her eye and slid down her cheek. "You almost did. How about you don't ever, *ever* do that again?"

He wouldn't make any promises. When it came to Noelle, he'd do anything if it meant she was alive and happy. Her hand still held his. He lifted their joined hands, ignoring the slight burn of the IV, and he pressed a kiss to the back of her hand.

"I love you." Saying the words to her seemed as natural as breathing. He'd never given those words to another woman, and Thomas knew

Noelle would be the only one he ever did say them to. She'd held his heart for so long. Her courage had drawn him in. Her intelligence. Her goodness, which seemed to shine from within her. After spending so much time in the shadows and in the darkness, he'd been drawn to the light that was Noelle.

To him, she was… Hell, she was everything.

"Marry me."

Not the most suave of proposals.

But—

"Yes."

The machines around him raced, and Noelle pushed closer to him. "I don't want to spend my life without you, Thomas. I don't want to be alone anymore. I want *you*."

She was all he'd ever need.

His dreams. His hopes.

His.

Noelle pressed a kiss to his lips once more, and Thomas knew he was the luckiest damn man on earth.

Yeah, she was an angel, all right, and she was *his*.

Chapter Twelve

Noelle entered the interrogation room with slow, determined steps. Her heels clicked softly on the floor as she made her way toward the prisoner.

The woman sat at the table, a guard stationed behind her. The woman's blond hair had lost some of its polished shine, and the long locks were pulled back into a limp ponytail.

As Noelle drew closer to the table, Paula Quinn glanced up, a smile on her face. "So, I finally merited an audience, huh?"

Noelle didn't speak.

"Too bad about your partner..." Paula leaned forward. "I was out of my mind when I fired that shot, of course. Patrick had kidnapped me, and I—I just snapped."

Cry me a river. Noelle didn't believe the woman's lies for a moment.

"I was aiming for Patrick. Not the agent." Paula's voice lowered with what sounded like sorrow. "I'm so sorry that Agent Anthony died…"

The door opened behind Noelle. She didn't glance back. She didn't need to. Shock swept over Paula's face when she saw the identity of her second visitor.

"Agent Anthony isn't dead," Noelle said. She also didn't think Thomas should be back to work, but since he wasn't *technically* in the field, Mercer had given the clear for him to come in on the interrogation.

Noelle was back to working as a liaison, at least until the situation with Paula Quill was resolved. Mercer wanted the woman to break, and Noelle was about to make that happen.

Then, when the case was officially closed, she had a wedding to plan. After all, a woman had her priorities. And getting hitched to Thomas—definite priority. But, sending this killer in front of her to jail for the rest of Paula's life? *Current goal.*

This was the woman who'd nearly taken Thomas away from Noelle. Damn straight she was going to do everything possible to break Paula.

Noelle sat in front of Paula. Thomas pulled out the chair right beside her. He didn't even wince when he sat down. The guy was far too good at camouflaging his pain.

"He's alive!" A wide smile broke over Paula's face. She lifted her hands, showing the cuffs that circled her wrists. "I'm so glad! I never meant to shoot you. I meant to shoot—"

"Me?" Noelle finished softly.

The smile slipped from Paula's face. "Of course not! I was aiming for Patrick."

"But in order to get to him—" Thomas's voice cut like a knife "—you were ready to shoot through Noelle."

Noelle slanted a quick glance his way. Did he even realize his voice had softened when he said her name? That had been...sweet. As sweet as she knew Thomas would ever get while they were at the EOD. After all, the man had an image to maintain.

"I—I was so scared..." Paula's shoulders shook.

Paula really was a terrific actress.

Noelle reached for the files that were waiting on the table. She flipped them open. "You started working for Senator Duncan over ten years ago."

"Ah...yes. Yes, I did..."

"And when you mention Patrick Porter, you always use his first name... That's an intimate association, so I assume you met him over the years while you were working with the senator?"

Paula's gaze darted to Thomas, then back to Noelle. "Patrick would come to see the senator every few months. They were friends." Her breath huffed out. "I can't believe that he killed him! And then abducted me!"

"Oh, I think you can believe it," Thomas muttered.

Paula's stare hardened for an instant.

Noelle asked, "You weren't aware that Patrick was killing for the senator?"

As Noelle stared at Paula, the other woman's mouth dropped open in a perfect O of surprise. "You can't be serious! There's no way—"

"Oh, I'm serious. You deleted the record of the kills from the senator's computer, but you weren't quite good enough at that deletion. We've got computer techs here… They can recover *anything* if you just give them time." Noelle smiled at Paula. "Serial killers like to keep souvenirs of their kills, did you know that? Patrick… His thing was pictures. Videos. When he had completed a kill, he'd send that image to Lawrence as proof the job was done. It was all of those images that you tried to delete. The video files."

Paula shook her head. "I have *no* idea what you're talking about!"

She could keep up the lies for a bit longer.

"The files were deleted *after* the senator's death."

"Then Patrick must've done it! He got into the system and—"

Noelle shook her head. "The only fingerprints on that keyboard were yours and the senator's."

Paula flushed. Her cuffed hands slammed against the table. "Then he used gloves. I don't know—"

"I think you know plenty," Thomas drawled as he leaned forward, "because you were featured in some of those videos." He reached for the laptop on the table. "Want to see them?"

Paula's face changed then. The pretty veneer faded. Evil flashed in her eyes.

"Patrick liked to work with a partner, and Lawrence, well, he was the more hands-off kind of guy, right?" Noelle asked, her voice emotionless. "So you were the one who went in with Patrick. The one who helped him lure those victims out. For the past ten years, Patrick had been killing men. The high-profile enemies of the senator. And to lure out prey like that…"

"You need the right bait," Thomas finished.

Bait that looked innocent but wasn't. Bait that would be too seductive to resist.

Thomas tapped a few buttons on the keyboard. A video began to play. Paula's soft laughter filled the room. Only this time, that laughter was coming from the recording. The woman was as still as a statue across from them as her eyes locked on the screen.

"Stop it," Paula whispered.

They didn't stop the video.

"I'm so glad we decided to get away for the weekend..." Now a man's deep, rumbling voice came from that video. *"Leaving D.C. was the best idea you've had..."*

"That's General Randall Adams. He worked for the Pentagon." Noelle shrugged. "You know that, though, right? Since the two of you were lovers. Randall's the one who first tipped you off about the EOD. You worried the EOD was closing in on you and Lawrence, that we'd realize—"

"I don't know anything about the EOD," Paula said, the words quiet but hard.

Thomas drummed his fingers on the table. "Once you came up on the EOD's radar, you knew we'd realize you'd been killing for years. We go after threats to security, and that's exactly what you are."

The video kept playing.

"Sometimes, Paula," Randall murmured, *"I wish you and I could give it all up. Just be together..."*

Paula's cuffed hands grabbed for the laptop. She shoved the top down. "I don't want to see anymore."

Noelle realized she'd been right. Of all the clips on that laptop, and there were plenty, the one of Randall had been the one Paula needed to see. "When Patrick kills him later—and Randall certainly wasn't easy to kill—your name is the last thing the general says."

The color was completely gone from Paula's face. Her lips twisted into a snarl. "Pointing at his accuser, is he?"

Thomas's fingers stilled on the table. "No, I think he was just calling out for the woman he loved."

Noelle turned her head to look at his hard profile.

"In those lasts minutes, you know what really matters," Thomas continued. His gaze flickered to Noelle. "You want to be clear, no words left unsaid, before you draw that last breath."

A sob broke from Paula.

Noelle had to swallow to clear the lump from her own throat. She could still hear Thomas's rough growl in her ears. *"I...love you..."*

"It was all Lawrence!" Paula said in a rush. "He's the one who made me work with Patrick! He found out that I'd killed my stepfather when I was sixteen." Tears trekked down her cheeks, but they weren't fake any longer. "He was hurting me, and I stopped him. No one would believe my stories about my stepfather, so I had to do something!" Shudders shook her. "Then Lawrence came along.... I—I thought he was going to help me, but he had other plans. Everyone always does...."

"Everyone but Randall," Noelle said softly.

Paula's shoulders bowed. "Lawrence flipped out when we got confirmation from Randall about the EOD. He was sure someone there— someone called Mercer—would be coming after him. That all the dots from his crimes would be connected. So, yes, he went after them. He didn't want the hit coming right back to him and Patrick, so he hired some guy for the job."

Jack.

"But since I'm here...and they're all dead..." Paula blinked away tears. "I guess the EOD didn't end, did it? Mercer... He's not dead."

Thomas pushed away from the table. The legs of his chair groaned. He headed for the door.

Noelle sat at the table for a moment longer. His job was finished. Hers wasn't. Now she needed to get the rest of the details. Names and dates. Closure would be given to families, and if Noelle's instincts were right, they would even get new leads to follow based on the information Paula would give them. Paula had been deeply connected in the senator's life. If there were others who'd tried to hide secrets in D.C., then Paula would know about them.

The woman would cooperate now. There was no reason for her not to do so.

The door closed softly behind Thomas.

Noelle stared at Paula.

"I loved him," Paula whispered.

Noelle reached for a pen and a pad.

"I loved him," Paula said again. "And after Randall was dead...I—I wanted to be, too...."

THOMAS HEADED INTO the next room. He shut the door behind him. Mercer was standing at attention, just a few feet away from the observation window that let him watch Noelle and Paula.

"The EOD isn't dead," Mercer said voice curt. "And we won't ever be. No matter how many times they come after us." He turned, focusing on Thomas. "Because of men like you. Women like Noelle. Agents who will risk their lives to protect the division."

It wasn't the division Thomas had thought of when he'd leapt to take that bullet in Alaska. It was the only woman he'd ever loved. "I'm marrying her."

Mercer's left eyebrow shot up. "Does Noelle know? Or is this some—"

"Noelle knows I love her, and she's agreed to marry me." *And I know just how lucky I am.* "I won't have any more secrets between us. Not ever again." He was giving that warning to Mercer.

"Good. That's the way it should be."

"Sir—"

Mercer lifted a hand. "My agents sacrifice for the EOD. You think I don't know that?" And, for an instant, the mask Mercer usually wore fell away. "They give up their homes, their families... They focus on the missions. But life is more than just a mission." He came forward and slapped a hand on Thomas's shoulder. "A whole lot more, and I'm glad you finally realized that."

Thomas glanced toward the observation glass. Noelle was questioning Paula, and Paula was telling her everything.

But his gaze wasn't on the captured woman. It was on Noelle. He could see the side of her face. The soft profile. The delicate line of her jaw.

"I knew you loved her," Mercer told him gruffly. "I just wondered when you'd realize it yourself."

Those words had Thomas's stare jerking back toward his boss.

Mercer smiled. *Smiled.* "It's in how you look at her. Usually, you stare at the world as if daring someone to attack you. But you stare at her…" He exhaled and his hand dropped from Thomas's shoulder. "You stare at her as if it's Christmas morning, and you just found the presents beneath the tree."

Thomas swallowed. "She's what matters most to me."

"Then she needs to be the one person you hold tightest." Mercer gave a firm nod. "Don't let her go, and, son, you don't hesitate to tell that woman how you feel every single day of your life." For an instant, sadness flashed in his eyes. "Because the days pass too fast, and you never know when you could wake up and find—" Mercer broke off then. He turned away from Thomas. "Wait for Noelle to finish up the interview. When she's done, you two take the next week off. I think you've earned that time."

Mercer headed for the door.

Thomas didn't move from his spot in front of the observation window. When the door shut behind Mercer, Thomas kept watching Noelle.

He knew what Mercer had been about to say. *You never know when you could wake up and find her gone.*

Yes, he knew about the director's past. Because he knew most of the secrets at the EOD. Once upon a time, Mercer had loved, too. But his wife had been taken from him.

You never know when you could wake up and find her gone.

Noelle turned her head then and looked toward the observation room. He stared into her eyes. The most gorgeous eyes he'd ever seen.

He wouldn't think of a life without Noelle. She'd been the one thing to get him through the darkest times of his life. No matter what hellhole he'd entered, she'd been there, the light in the darkness. The image of her had gotten him through so many times when he thought escape would be impossible.

No, he wouldn't think of a life without her. Because he didn't want to live that life.

He had his dream, he had Noelle, and Thomas knew he would fight heaven and hell to keep her by his side.

He stayed there, watching, until the interrogation was over, and when Noelle finally came into the room to find him, Thomas stalked toward her.

"Thomas?"

He pulled her into his arms. He still didn't think she realized just how incredibly important she was to him. Maybe one day, she would.

"I love you." The words came from him so easily now. No stumbles. No hesitations.

She smiled.

For so long, darkness had been all he'd known. But not any longer. Now he had light.

He had love.

He had Noelle.

Thomas kissed her.

* * * * *

LARGER-PRINT BOOKS!

GET 2 FREE LARGER-PRINT NOVELS PLUS

2 FREE GIFTS!

⚜ HARLEQUIN®

Romance

From the Heart, For the Heart

ReaderService.com

Manage your account online!

- Review your order history
- Manage your payments
- Update your address

---

*We've designed
the Harlequin® Reader Service
website just for you.*

Enjoy all the features!

- Reader excerpts from any series
- Respond to mailings and
  special monthly offers
- Discover new series available to you
- Browse the Bonus Bucks catalog
- Share your feedback

Visit us at:

ReaderService.com